THE MOST FAMOUS TRIUMPH OF THE WORLD'S MOST RENOWNED MYSTERY WRITER

Witness for the Prosecution was made into a great stage success and an unforgettable motion picture. But none of these versions could match the original of this fantastically intriguing courtroom drama for nerve-twisting suspense and startling turnabout.

Now this great tale appears with eight other superlative spellbinders that exhibit the full range of Agatha Christie's remarkable talents, from eerie horror to brain-teasing bafflement—with the vivid characters and ingenious solutions that have made the author the first-ranked mystery writer in the entire world.

You will never guess the ending of—

WITNESS FOR THE PROSECUTION

WITNESS For The PROSECUTION

●

Agatha Christie

A DELL BOOK

Published by
DELL PUBLISHING CO., INC.
750 Third Avenue
New York, New York 10017
© Copyright 1924, 1926, 1929, 1944, 1947, 1948,
by Agatha Christie
© Copyright 1932, by The Curtis Publishing Company
Dell ® TM 681510, Dell Publishing Co., Inc.
Reprinted by arrangement with
Dodd, Mead & Company, Inc.
New York, New York
The characters, places, incidents and situations
in this book are imaginary and have no relation
to any person, place or actual happening.
Printed in the United States of America
Previous Dell Edition #9619
New Dell Edition
First printing—April 1972

THE WITNESS FOR THE PROSECUTION

Mr. Mayherne adjusted his pince-nez and cleared his throat with a little dry-as-dust cough that was wholly typical of him. Then he looked again at the man opposite him, the man charged with willful murder.

Mr. Mayherne was a small man, precise in manner, neatly, not to say foppishly dressed, with a pair of very shrewd and piercing gray eyes. By no means a fool. Indeed, as a solicitor, Mr. Mayherne's reputation stood very high. His voice, when he spoke to his client, was dry but not unsympathetic.

"I must impress upon you again that you are in very grave danger, and that the utmost frankness is necessary."

Leonard Vole, who had been staring in a dazed fashion at the blank wall in front of him, transferred his glance to the solicitor.

"I know," he said hopelessly. "You keep telling me so. But I can't seem to realize yet that I'm charged with murder—*murder*. And such a dastardly crime, too."

Mr. Mayherne was practical, not emotional. He coughed again, took off his pince-nez, polished them carefully, and replaced them on his nose. Then he said, "Yes, yes, yes. Now, my dear Mr. Vole, we're going to make a determined effort to get you off—and we shall succeed—we shall succeed. But I must have all the facts. I must know just how damaging the case against you is likely to be. Then we can fix upon the best line of defense."

Still the young man looked at him in the same dazed, hopeless fashion. To Mr. Mayherne the case had seemed black enough, and the guilt of the prisoner assured. Now, for the first time, he felt a doubt.

"You think I'm guilty," said Leonard Vole, in a low

voice. "But, by God, I swear I'm not! It looks pretty black against me, I know that. I'm like a man caught in a net—the meshes of it all round me, entangling me whichever way I turn. But I didn't do it, Mr. Mayherne, I didn't do it!"

In such a position a man was bound to protest his innocence. Mr. Mayherne knew that. Yet, in spite of himself, he was impressed. It might be, after all, that Leonard Vole was innocent.

"You are right, Mr. Vole," he said gravely. "The case does look very black against you. Nevertheless, I accept your assurance. Now, let us get to facts. I want you to tell me in your own words exactly how you came to make the acquaintance of Miss Emily French."

"It was one day in Oxford Street. I saw an elderly lady crossing the road. She was carrying a lot of parcels. In the middle of the street she dropped them, tried to recover them, found a bus was almost on top of her, and just managed to reach the curb safely, dazed and bewildered by people having shouted at her. I recovered her parcels, wiped the mud off them as best I could, retied the string of one, and returned them to her."

"There was no question of your having saved her life?"

"Oh, dear me, no! All I did was to perform a common act of courtesy. She was extremely grateful, thanked me warmly, and said something about my manners not being those of most of the younger generation—I can't remember the exact words. Then I lifted my hat and went on. I never expected to see her again. But life is full of coincidences. That very evening I came across her at a party at a friend's house. She recognized me at once and asked that I should be introduced to her. I then found out that she was a Miss Emily French and that she lived at Cricklewood. I talked to her for some time. She was, I imagine, an old lady who took sudden and violent fancies to people. She took one to me on the strength of a perfectly simple action which anyone might have performed. On leaving, she shook me warmly by the hand and asked me to come and see her. I replied, of course, that I should be very pleased to do so, and she then urged me to name a day. I did not want particularly to go, but it would have seemed churlish to refuse, so I fixed on the following Saturday. After she had gone, I learned something about her from my friends. That she was rich, eccentric, lived alone with one maid, and owned no less than eight cats."

"I see," said Mr. Mayherne. "The question of her being well off came up as early as that?"

"If you mean that I inquired—" began Leonard Vole hotly, but Mr. Mayherne stilled him with a gesture.

"I have to look at the case as it will be presented by the other side. An ordinary observer would not have supposed Miss French to be a lady of means. She lived poorly, almost humbly. Unless you had been told the contrary, you would in all probability have considered her to be in poor circumstances—at any rate to begin with. Who was it exactly who told you that she was well off?"

"My friend, George Harvey, at whose house the party took place."

"Is he likely to remember having done so?"

"I really don't know. Of course it is some time ago now."

"Quite so, Mr. Vole. You see, the first aim of the prosecution will be to establish that you were in low water financially—that is true, is it not?"

Leonard Vole flushed.

"Yes," he said, in a low voice. "I'd been having a run of infernal bad luck just then."

"Quite so," said Mr. Mayherne again. "That being, as I say, in low water financially, you met this rich old lady and cultivated her acquaintance assiduously. Now if we are in a position to say that you had no idea she was well off, and that you visited her out of pure kindness of heart—"

"Which is the case."

"I dare say. I am not disputing the point. I am looking

at it from the outside point of view. A great deal depends on the memory of Mr. Harvey. Is he likely to remember that conversation or is he not? Could he be confused by counsel into believing that it took place later?"

Leonard Vole reflected for some minutes. Then he said steadily enough, but with a rather pale face, "I do not think that that line would be successful, Mr. Mayherne. Several of those present heard his remark, and one or two of them chaffed me about my conquest of a rich old lady."

The solicitor endeavored to hide his disappointment with a wave of the hand.

"Unfortunate," he said. "But I congratulate you upon your plain speaking, Mr. Vole. It is to you I look to guide me. Your judgment is quite right. To persist in the line I spoke of would have been disastrous. We must leave that point. You made the acquaintance of Miss French, you called upon her, the acquaintanceship progressed. We want a clear reason for all this. Why did you, a young man of thirty-three, good-looking, fond of sport, popular with your friends, devote so much of your time to an elderly woman with whom you could hardly have anything in common?"

Leonard Vole flung out his hands in a nervous gesture.

"I can't tell you—I really can't tell you. After the first visit, she pressed me to come again, spoke of being lonely and unhappy. She made it difficult for me to refuse. She showed so plainly her fondness and affection for me that I was placed in an awkward position. You see, Mr. Mayherne, I've got a weak nature—I drift—I'm one of those people who can't say no. And believe me or not, as you like, after the third or fourth visit I paid her I found myself getting genuinely fond of the old thing. My mother died when I was young, an aunt brought me up, and she, too, died before I was fifteen. If I told you that I genuinely enjoyed being mothered and pampered, I dare say you'd only laugh."

Mr. Mayherne did not laugh. Instead he took off his pince-nez again and polished them, a sign with him that he was thinking deeply.

"I accept your explanation, Mr. Vole," he said at last. "I believe it to be psychologically probable. Whether a jury would take that view of it is another matter. Please continue your narrative. When was it that Miss French first asked you to look into her business affairs?"

"After my third or fourth visit to her. She understood very little of money matters, and was worried about some investments."

Mr. Mayherne looked up sharply.

"Be careful, Mr. Vole. The maid, Janet Mackenzie, declares that her mistress was a good woman of business and transacted all her own affairs, and this is borne out by the testimony of her bankers."

"I can't help that," said Vole earnestly. "That's what she said to me."

Mr. Mayherne looked at him for a moment or two in silence. Though he had no intention of saying so, his belief in Leonard Vole's innocence was at that moment strengthened. He knew something of the mentality of elderly ladies. He saw Miss French, infatuated with the good-looking young man, hunting about for pretexts that would bring him to the house. What more likely than that she should plead ignorance of business, and beg him to help her with her money affairs? She was enough of a woman of the world to realize that any man is slightly flattered by such an admission of his superiority. Leonard Vole had been flattered. Perhaps, too, she had not been averse to letting this young man know that she was wealthy. Emily French had been a strong-willed old woman, willing to pay her price for what she wanted. All this passed rapidly through Mr. Mayherne's mind, but he gave no indication of it, and asked instead a further question.

"And did you handle her affairs for her at her request?"

"I did."

"Mr. Vole," said the solicitor, "I am going to ask you a very serious question, and one to which it is vital I should have a truthful answer. You were in low water financially. You had the handling of an old lady's affairs—an old lady who, according to her own statement, knew little or nothing of business. Did you at any time, or in any manner, convert to your own use the securities which you handled? Did you engage in any transaction for your own pecuniary advantage which will not bear the light of day?" He quelled the other's response. "Wait a minute before you answer. There are two courses open to us. Either we can make a feature of your probity and honesty in conducting her affairs while pointing out how unlikely it is that you would commit murder to obtain money which you might have obtained by such infinitely easier means. If, on the other hand, there is anything in your dealings which the prosecution will get hold of—if, to put it baldly, it can be proved that you swindled the old lady in any way, we must take the line that you had no motive for the murder, since she was already a profitable source of income to you. You perceive the distinction. Now, I beg of you, take your time before you reply."

But Leonard Vole took no time at all.

"My dealings with Miss French's affairs were all perfectly fair and above board. I acted for her interests to the very best of my ability, as anyone will find who looks into the matter."

"Thank you," said Mr. Mayherne. "You relieve my mind very much. I pay you the compliment of believing that you are far too clever to lie to me over such an important matter."

"Surely," said Vole eagerly, "the strongest point in my favor is the lack of motive. Granted that I cultivated the acquaintanceship of a rich old lady in the hopes of getting money out of her—that, I gather, is the substance of what you have been saying—surely her death frustrates all my hopes?"

The solicitor looked at him steadily. Then, very deliberately, he repeated his unconscious trick with his pince-nez. It was not until they were firmly replaced on his nose that he spoke.

"Are you not aware, Mr. Vole, that Miss French left a will under which you are the principal beneficiary?"

"What?" The prisoner sprang to his feet. His dismay was obvious and unforced. "My God! What are you saying? She left her money to me?"

Mr. Mayherne nodded slowly. Vole sank down again, his head in his hands.

"You pretend you know nothing of this will?"

"Pretend? There's no pretense about it. I knew nothing about it."

"What would you say if I told you that the maid, Janet Mackenzie, swears that you *did* know? That her mistress told her distinctly that she had consulted you in the matter, and told you of her intentions?"

"Say? That she's lying! No, I go too fast. Janet is an elderly woman. She was a faithful watchdog to her mistress, and she didn't like me. She was jealous and suspicious. I should say that Miss French confided her intentions to Janet, and that Janet either mistook something she said, or else was convinced in her own mind that I had persuaded the old lady into doing it. I dare say that she herself believes now that Miss French actually told her so."

"You don't think she dislikes you enough to lie deliberately about the matter?"

Leonard Vole looked shocked and startled.

"No, indeed! Why should she?"

"I don't know," said Mr. Mayherne thoughtfully. "But she's very bitter against you."

The wretched young man groaned again.

"I'm beginning to see," he muttered. "It's frightful. I

made up to her, that's what they'll say, I got her to make a will leaving her money to me, and then I go there that night, and there's nobody in the house—they find her the next day—oh, my God, it's awful!"

"You are wrong about there being nobody in the house," said Mr. Mayherne. "Janet, as you remember, was to go out for the evening. She went, but about half past nine she returned to fetch the pattern of a blouse sleeve which she had promised to a friend. She let herself in by the back door, went upstairs and fetched it, and went out again. She heard voices in the sitting-room, though she could not distinguish what they said, but she will swear that one of them was Miss French's and one was a man's."

"At half past nine," said Leonard Vole. "At half past nine—" He sprang to his feet. "But then I'm saved—saved—"

"What do you mean, saved?" cried Mr. Mayherne, astonished.

"By half past nine I was at home again! My wife can prove that. I left Miss French about five minutes to nine. I arrived home about twenty past nine. My wife was there waiting for me. Oh, thank God—thank God! And bless Janet Mackenzie's sleeve pattern."

In his exuberance, he hardly noticed that the grave expression on the solicitor's face had not altered. But the latter's words brought him down to earth with a bump.

"Who, then, in your opinion, murdered Miss French?"

"Why, a burglar, of course, as was thought at first. The window was forced, you remember. She was killed with a heavy blow from a crowbar, and the crowbar was found lying on the floor beside the body. And several articles were missing. But for Janet's absurd suspicions and dislike of me, the police would never have swerved from the right track."

"That will hardly do, Mr. Vole," said the solicitor. "The things that were missing were mere trifles of no value, taken as a blind. And the marks on the window were not at all conclusive. Besides, think for yourself. You say you were no longer in the house by half past nine. Who, then, was the man Janet heard talking to Miss French in the sitting-room? She would hardly be having an amicable conversation with a burglar."

"No," said Vole. "No—" He looked puzzled and discouraged. "But, anyway," he added with reviving spirit, "it lets me out. I've got an alibi. You must see Romaine—my wife —at once."

"Certainly," acquiesced the lawyer. "I should already have seen Mrs. Vole but for her being absent when you were arrested. I wired to Scotland at once, and I understand that she arrives back tonight. I am going to call upon her immediately I leave here."

Vole nodded, a great expression of satisfaction settling down over his face.

"Yes, Romaine will tell you. My God! it's a lucky chance that."

"Excuse me, Mr. Vole, but you are very fond of your wife?"

"Of course."

"And she of you?"

"Romaine is devoted to me. She'd do anything in the world for me."

He spoke enthusiastically, but the solicitor's heart sank a little lower. The testimony of a devoted wife—would it gain credence?

"Was there anyone else who saw you return at nine-twenty. A maid, for instance?"

"We have no maid."

"Did you meet anyone in the street on the way back?"

"Nobody I knew. I rode part of the way in a bus. The conductor might remember."

Mr. Mayherne shook his head doubtfully.

"There is no one, then, who can confirm your wife's testimony?"

"No. But it isn't necessary, surely?"

"I dare say not. I dare say not," said Mr. Mayherne hastily. "Now there's just one thing more. Did Miss French know that you were a married man?"

"Oh, yes."

"Yet you never took your wife to see her. Why was that?"

For the first time, Leonard Vole's answer came halting and uncertain.

"Well—I don't know."

"Are you aware that Janet Mackenzie says her mistress believed you to be single, and contemplated marrying you in the future?"

Vole laughed. "Absurd! There was forty years' difference in age between us."

"It has been done," said the solicitor dryly. "The fact remains. Your wife never met Miss French?"

"No—" Again the constraint.

"You will permit me to say," said the lawyer, "that I hardly understand your attitude in the matter."

Vole flushed, hesitated, and then spoke.

"I'll make a clean breast of it. I was hard up, as you know. I hoped that Miss French might lend me some money. She was fond of me, but she wasn't at all interested in the struggles of a young couple. Early on, I found that she had taken it for granted that my wife and I didn't get on—were living apart. Mr. Mayherne—I wanted the money—for Romaine's sake. I said nothing, and allowed the old lady to think what she chose. She spoke of my being an adopted son to her. There was never any question of marriage—that must be just Janet's imagination."

"And that is all?"

"Yes—that is all."

Was there just a shade of hesitation in the words? The lawyer fancied so. He rose and held out his hand.

"Good-by, Mr. Vole." He looked into the haggard young face and spoke with an unusual impulse. "I believe in your innocence in spite of the multitude of facts arrayed against you. I hope to prove it and vindicate you completely."

Vole smiled back at him.

"You'll find the alibi is all right," he said cheerfully.

Again he hardly noticed that the other did not respond.

"The whole thing hinges a good deal on the testimony of Janet Mackenzie," said Mr. Mayherne. "She hates you. That much is clear."

"She can hardly hate me," protested the young man.

The solicitor shook his head as he went out. *Now for Mrs. Vole,* he said to himself. He was seriously disturbed by the way the thing was shaping.

The Voles lived in a small shabby house near Paddington Green. It was to this house that Mr. Mayherne went.

In answer to his ring, a big slatternly woman, obviously a charwoman, answered the door.

"Mrs. Vole? Has she returned yet?"

"Got back an hour ago. But I dunno if you can see her."

"If you will take my card to her," said Mr. Mayherne quietly, "I am quite sure that she will do so."

The woman looked at him doubtfully, wiped her hand on her apron, and took the card. Then she closed the door in his face and left him on the step outside.

In a few minutes, however, she returned with a slightly altered manner.

"Come inside, please."

She ushered him into a tiny drawing-room. Mr. Mayherne, examining a drawing on the wall, started up suddenly to face a tall, pale woman who had entered so quietly that he had not heard her.

"Mr. Mayherne? You are my husband's solicitor, are you not? You have come from him? Will you please sit down?"

Until she spoke he had not realized that she was not

English. Now, observing her more closely, he noticed the high cheekbones, the dense blue-black of the hair, and an occasional very slight movement of the hands that was distinctly foreign. A strange woman, very quiet. So quiet as to make one uneasy. From the very first Mr. Mayherne was conscious that he was up against something that he did not understand.

"Now, my dear Mrs. Vole," he began, "you must not give way—"

He stopped. It was so very obvious that Romaine Vole had not the slightest intention of giving way. She was perfectly calm and composed.

"Will you please tell me about it?" she said. "I must know everything. Do not think to spare me. I want to know the worst." She hesitated, then repeated in a lower tone, with a curious emphasis which the lawyer did not understand, "I want to know the worst."

Mr. Mayherne went over his interview with Leonard Vole. She listened attentively, nodding her head now and then.

"I see," she said, when he had finished. "He wants me to say that he came in at twenty minutes past nine that night?"

"He did come in at that time?" said Mr. Mayherne sharply.

"That is not the point," she said coldly. "Will my saying so acquit him? Will they believe me?"

Mr. Mayherne was taken aback. She had gone so quickly to the core of the matter.

"That is what I want to know," she said. "Will it be enough? Is there anyone else who can support my evidence?"

There was a suppressed eagerness in her manner that made him vaguely uneasy.

"So far there is no one else," he said reluctantly.

"I see," said Romaine Vole.

She sat for a minute or two perfectly still. A little smile played over her lips.

The lawyer's feeling of alarm grew stronger and stronger.

"Mrs. Vole—" he began. "I know what you must feel—"

"Do you?" she asked. "I wonder."

"In the circumstances—"

"In the circumstances—I intend to play a lone hand."

He looked at her in dismay.

"But, my dear Mrs. Vole—you are overwrought. Being so devoted to your husband—"

"I beg your pardon?"

The sharpness of her voice made him start. He repeated in a hesitating manner, "Being so devoted to your husband—"

Romaine Vole nodded slowly, the same strange smile on her lips.

"Did he tell you that I was devoted to him?" she asked softly. "Ah! yes, I can see he did. How stupid men are! Stupid—stupid—stupid—"

She rose suddenly to her feet. All the intense emotion that the lawyer had been conscious of in the atmosphere was now concentrated in her tone.

"I hate him, I tell you! I hate him. I hate him. I hate him! I would like to see him hanged by the neck till he is dead."

The lawyer recoiled before her and the smoldering passion in her eyes.

She advanced a step nearer and continued vehemently.

"Perhaps I shall see it. Supposing I tell you that he did not come in that night at twenty past nine, but at twenty past ten? You say that he tells you he knew nothing about the money coming to him. Supposing I tell you he knew all about it, and counted on it, and committed murder to get it? Supposing I tell you that he admitted to me that night when he came in what he had done? That there was blood on his coat? What then? Supposing that I stand up in court and say all these things?"

Her eyes seemed to challenge him. With an effort he concealed his growing dismay, and endeavored to speak in a rational tone.

"You cannot be asked to give evidence against your husband—"

"He is not my husband!"

The words came out so quickly that he fancied he had misunderstood her.

"I beg your pardon? I—"

"He is not my husband."

The silence was so intense that you could have heard a pin drop.

"I was an actress in Vienna. My husband is alive but in a madhouse. So we could not marry. I am glad now." She nodded defiantly.

"I should like you to tell me one thing," said Mr. Mayherne. He contrived to appear as cool and unemotional as ever. "Why are you so bitter against Leonard Vole?"

She shook her head, smiling a little.

"Yes, you would like to know. But I shall not tell you. I will keep my secret."

Mr. Mayherne gave his dry little cough and rose.

"There seems no point in prolonging this interview," he remarked. "You will hear from me again after I have communicated with my client."

She came closer to him, looking into his eyes with her own wonderful dark ones.

"Tell me," she said, "did you believe—honestly—that he was innocent when you came here today?"

"I did," said Mr. Mayherne.

"You poor little man." She laughed.

"And I believe so still," finished the lawyer. "Good evening, madam."

He went out of the room, taking with him the memory

of her startled face. *This is going to be the devil of a business,* said Mr. Mayherne to himself as he strode along the street.

Extraordinary, the whole thing. An extraordinary woman. A very dangerous woman. Women were the devil when they got their knife into you.

What was to be done? That wretched young man hadn't a leg to stand upon. Of course, possibly he did commit the crime.

No, said Mr. Mayherne to himself. *No—there's almost too much evidence against him. I don't believe this woman. She was trumping up the whole story. But she'll never bring it into court.*

He wished he felt more conviction on the point.

The police court proceedings were brief and dramatic. The principal witnesses for the prosecution were Janet Mackenzie, maid to the dead woman, and Romaine Heilger, Austrian subject, the mistress of the prisoner.

Mr. Mayherne sat in court and listened to the damning story that the latter told. It was on the lines she had indicated to him in their interview.

The prisoner reserved his defense and was committed for trial.

Mr. Mayherne was at his wits' end. The case against Leonard Vole was black beyond words. Even the famous K.C. who was engaged for the defense held out little hope.

"If we can shake that Austrian woman's testimony, we might do something," he said dubiously. "But it's a bad business."

Mr. Mayherne had concentrated his energies on one single point. Assuming Leonard Vole to be speaking the truth, and to have left the murdered woman's house at nine o'clock, who was the man Janet heard talking to Miss French at half past nine?

The only ray of light was in the shape of a scapegrace

nephew who had in bygone days cajoled and threatened his aunt out of various sums of money. Janet Mackenzie, the solicitor learned, had always been attached to this young man, and had never ceased urging his claims upon her mistress. It certainly seemed possible that it was this nephew who had been with Miss French after Leonard Vole left, especially as he was not to be found in any of his old haunts.

In all other directions, the lawyer's researches had been negative in their result. No one had seen Leonard Vole entering his own house, or leaving that of Miss French. No one had seen any other man enter or leave the house in Cricklewood. All inquiries drew blank.

It was the eve of the trial when Mr. Mayherne received the letter which was to lead his thoughts in an entirely new direction.

It came by the six-o'clock post. An illiterate scrawl, written on common paper and enclosed in a dirty envelope with the stamp stuck on crooked.

Mr. Mayherne read it through once or twice before he grasped its meaning.

Dear Mister:
Youre the lawyer chap wot acts for the young feller. If you want that painted foreign hussy showd up for wot she is an her pack of lies you come to 16 Shaw's Rents Stepney to-night It ull cawst you 2 hundred quid Arsk for Missis Mogson.

The solicitor read and reread this strange epistle. It might, of course, be a hoax, but when he thought it over, he became increasingly convinced that it was genuine, and also convinced that it was the one hope for the prisoner. The evidence of Romaine Heilger damned him completely, and the line the defense meant to pursue, the line that the evidence of a woman who had admittedly lived an immoral life was not to be trusted, was at best a weak one.

Mr. Mayherne's mind was made up. It was his duty to save his client at all costs. He must go to Shaw's Rents.

He had some difficulty in finding the place, a ramshackle building in an evil-smelling slum, but at last he did so, and on inquiry for Mrs. Mogson was sent up to a room on the third floor. On this door he knocked, and getting no answer, knocked again.

At this second knock, he heard a shuffling sound inside, and presently the door was opened cautiously half an inch and a bent figure peered out.

Suddenly the woman, for it was a woman, gave a chuckle and opened the door wider.

"So it's you, dearie," she said, in a wheezy voice. "Nobody with you, is there? No playing tricks? That's right. You can come in—you can come in."

With some reluctance the lawyer stepped across the threshold into the small, dirty room, with its flickering gas jet. There was an untidy unmade bed in a corner, a plain deal table, and two rickety chairs. For the first time Mr. Mayherne had a full view of the tenant of this unsavory apartment. She was a woman of middle age, bent in figure, with a mass of untidy gray hair and a scarf wound tightly round her face. She saw him looking at this and laughed again, the same curious, toneless chuckle.

"Wondering why I hide my beauty, dear? He, he, he. Afraid it may tempt you, eh? But you shall see—you shall see."

She drew aside the scarf, and the lawyer recoiled involuntarily before the almost formless blur of scarlet. She replaced the scarf again.

"So you're not wanting to kiss me, dearie? He, he, I don't wonder. And yet I was a pretty girl once—not so long ago as you'd think, either. Vitriol, dearie, vitriol—that's what did that. Ah! but I'll be even with 'em—"

She burst into a hideous torrent of profanity which Mr. Mayherne tried vainly to quell. She fell silent at last, her hands clenching and unclenching themselves nervously.

"Enough of that," said the lawyer sternly. "I've come here because I have reason to believe you can give me information which will clear my client, Leonard Vole. Is that the case?"

Her eyes leered at him cunningly.

"What about the money, dearie?" she wheezed. "Two hundred quid, you remember."

"It is your duty to give evidence, and you can be called upon to do so."

"That won't do, dearie. I'm an old woman, and I know nothing. But you give me two hundred quid, and perhaps I can give you a hint or two. See?"

"What kind of hint?"

"What should you say to a letter? A letter from *her*. Never mind how I got hold of it. That's my business. It'll do the trick. But I want my two hundred quid."

Mr. Mayherne looked at her coldly, and made up his mind.

"I'll give you ten pounds, nothing more. And only that if this letter is what you say it is."

"Ten pounds?" She screamed and raved at him.

"Twenty," said Mr. Mayherne, "and that's my last word."

He rose as if to go. Then, watching her closely, he drew out a pocketbook, and counted out twenty one-pound notes.

"You see," he said. "That is all I have with me. You can take it or leave it."

But already he knew that the sight of the money was too much for her. She cursed and raved impotently, but at last she gave in. Going over to the bed, she drew something out from beneath the tattered mattress.

"Here you are, damn you!" she snarled. "It's the top

one you want."

It was a bundle of letters that she threw to him, and Mr. Mayherne untied them and scanned them in his usual cool, methodical manner. The woman, watching him eagerly, could gain no clue from his impassive face.

He read each letter through, then returned again to the top one and read it a second time. Then he tied the whole bundle up again carefully.

They were love letters, written by Romaine Heilger, and the man they were written to was not Leonard Vole. The top letter was dated the day of the latter's arrest.

"I spoke true, dearie, didn't I?" whined the woman. "It'll do for her, that letter?"

Mr. Mayherne put the letters in his pocket, then he asked a question.

"How did you get hold of this correspondence?"

"That's telling," she said with a leer. "But I know something more. I heard in court what that hussy said. Find out where she was at twenty past ten, the time she says she was at home. Ask at the Lion Road Cinema. They'll remember—a fine upstanding girl like that—curse her!"

"Who is the man?" asked Mr. Mayherne. "There's only a Christian name here."

The other's voice grew thick and hoarse, her hands clenched and unclenched. Finally she lifted one to her face.

"He's the man that did this to me. Many years ago now. She took him away from me—a chit of a girl she was then. And when I went after him—and went for him, too—he threw the cursed stuff at me! And she laughed—damn her! I've had it in for her for years. Followed her, I have, spied upon her. And now I've got her! She'll suffer for this, won't she, Mr. Lawyer? She'll suffer?"

"She will probably be sentenced to a term of imprisonment for perjury," said Mr. Mayherne quietly.

"Shut away—that's what I want. You're going, are you?

Where's my money? Where's that good money?"

Without a word, Mr. Mayherne put down the notes on the table. Then, drawing a deep breath, he turned and left the squalid room. Looking back, he saw the old woman crooning over the money.

He wasted no time. He found the cinema in Lion Road easily enough, and, shown a photograph of Romaine Heilger, the commissionaire recognized her at once. She had arrived at the cinema with a man some time after ten o'clock on the evening in question. He had not noticed her escort particularly, but he remembered the lady who had spoken to him about the picture that was showing. They stayed until the end, about an hour later.

Mr. Mayherne was satisfied. Romaine Heilger's evidence was a tissue of lies from beginning to end. She had evolved it out of her passionate hatred. The lawyer wondered whether he would ever know what lay behind that hatred. What had Leonard Vole done to her? He had seemed dumfounded when the solicitor had reported her attitude to him. He had declared earnestly that such a thing was incredible—yet it had seemed to Mr. Mayherne that after the first astonishment his protests had lacked sincerity.

He did know. Mr. Mayherne was convinced of it. He knew, but he had no intention of revealing the fact. The secret between those two remained a secret. Mr. Mayherne wondered if some day he should come to learn what it was.

The solicitor glanced at his watch. It was late, but time was everything. He hailed a taxi and gave an address.

"Sir Charles must know of this at once," he murmured to himself as he got in.

The trial of Leonard Vole for the murder of Emily French aroused widespread interest. In the first place the prisoner was young and good-looking, then he was accused of a particularly dastardly crime, and there was the further interest of Romaine Heilger, the principal witness for the prosecution. There had been pictures of her in many papers, and several fictitious stories as to her origin and history.

The proceedings opened quietly enough. Various technical evidence came first. Then Janet Mackenzie was called. She told substantially the same story as before. In cross-examination counsel for the defense succeeded in getting her to contradict herself once or twice over her account of Vole's association with Miss French; he emphasized the fact that though she had heard a man's voice in the sitting-room that night, there was nothing to show that it was Vole who was there, and he managed to drive home a feeling that jealousy and dislike of the prisoner were at the bottom of a good deal of her evidence.

Then the next witness was called.

"Your name is Romaine Heilger?"

"Yes."

"You are an Austrian subject?"

"Yes."

"For the last three years you have lived with the prisoner and passed yourself off as his wife?"

Just for a moment Romaine Heilger's eyes met those of the man in the dock. Her expression held something curious and unfathomable.

"Yes."

The questions went on. Word by word the damning facts came out. On the night in question the prisoner had taken out a crowbar with him. He had returned at twenty minutes past ten, and had confessed to having killed the old lady. His cuffs had been stained with blood, and he had burned them in the kitchen stove. He had terrorized her into silence by means of threats.

As the story proceeded, the feeling of the court which had, to begin with, been slightly favorable to the prisoner, now set dead against him. He himself sat with downcast head and moody air, as though he knew he were doomed.

Yet it might have been noted that her own counsel sought to restrain Romaine's animosity. He would have preferred her to be more unbiased.

Formidable and ponderous, counsel for the defense arose.

He put it to her that her story was a malicious fabrication from start to finish, that she had not even been in her own house at the time in question, that she was in love with another man and was deliberately seeking to send Vole to his death for a crime he did not commit.

Romaine denied these allegations with superb insolence.

Then came the surprising denouement, the production of the letter. It was read aloud in court in the midst of a breathless stillness.

"Max, beloved, the Fates have delivered him into our hands! He has been arrested for murder—but, yes, the murder of an old lady! Leonard, who would not hurt a fly! At last I shall have my revenge. The poor chicken! I shall say that he came in that night with blood upon him—that he confessed to me. I shall hang him, Max—and when he hangs he will know and realize that it was Romaine who sent him to his death. And then—happiness, Beloved! Happiness at last!"

There were experts present ready to swear that the handwriting was that of Romaine Heilger, but they were not needed. Confronted with the letter, Romaine broke down utterly and confessed everything. Leonard Vole had returned to the house at the time he said, twenty past nine. She had invented the whole story to ruin him.

With the collapse of Romaine Heilger, the case for the Crown collapsed also. Sir Charles called his few witnesses, the prisoner himself went into the box and told his story in a manly straightforward manner, unshaken by cross-examination.

The prosecution endeavored to rally, but without great success. The judge's summing up was not wholly favorable to the prisoner, but a reaction had set in and the jury needed little time to consider their verdict.

"We find the prisoner not guilty."

Leonard Vole was free!

Little Mr. Mayherne hurried from his seat. He must congratulate his client.

He found himself polishing his pince-nez vigorously, and checked himself. His wife had told him only the night before that he was getting a habit of it. Curious things, habits. People themselves never knew they had them.

An interesting case—a very interesting case. That woman, now, Romaine Heilger.

The case was dominated for him still by the exotic figure of Romaine Heilger. She had seemed a pale, quiet woman in the house at Paddington, but in court she had flamed out against the sober background, flaunting herself like a tropical flower.

If he closed his eyes he could see her now, tall and vehement, her exquisite body bent forward a little, her right hand clenching and unclenching itself unconsciously all the time.

Curious things, habits. That gesture of hers with the hand was her habit, he supposed. Yet he had seen someone else do it quite lately. Who was it now? Quite lately—

He drew in his breath with a gasp as it came back to him. The woman in Shaw's Rents—

He stood still, his head whirling. It was impossible— impossible— Yet, Romaine Heilger was an actress.

The K.C. came up behind him and clapped him on the shoulder.

"Congratulated our man yet? He's had a narrow shave, you know. Come along and see him."

But the little lawyer shook off the other's hand.

He wanted one thing only—to see Romaine Heilger face to face.

He did not see her until some time later, and the place of their meeting is not relevant.

"So you guessed," she said, when he had told her all that was in his mind. "The face? Oh! that was easy enough, and the light of that gas jet was too bad for you to see the make-up."

"But why—why—"

"Why did I play a lone hand?" She smiled a little, re-membering the last time she had used the words.

"Such an elaborate comedy!"

"My friend—I had to save him. The evidence of a woman devoted to him would not have been enough—you hinted as much yourself. But I know something of the psychology of crowds. Let my evidence be wrung from me, as an admission, damning me in the eyes of the law, and a reac-tion in favor of the prisoner would immediately set in."

"And the bundle of letters?"

"One alone, the vital one, might have seemed like a—what do you call it?—put-up job."

"Then the man called Max?"

"Never existed, my friend."

"I still think," said little Mr. Mayherne, in an aggrieved manner, "that we could have got him off by the—er—normal procedure."

"I dared not risk it. You see you thought he was inno-cent—"

"And you knew it? I see," said little Mr. Mayherne.

"My dear Mr. Mayherne," said Romaine, "you do not see at all. I knew—he was guilty!"

THE RED SIGNAL

"No, but how too thrilling," said pretty Mrs. Eversleigh, opening her lovely, but slightly vacant, blue eyes very wide. "They always say women have a sixth sense; do you think it's true, Sir Alington?"

The famous alienist smiled sardonically. He had an unbounded contempt for the foolish pretty type, such as his fellow guest. Alington West was the supreme authority on mental disease, and he was fully alive to his own position and importance. A slightly pompous man of full figure.

"A great deal of nonsense is talked, I know that, Mrs. Eversleigh. What does the term mean—a sixth sense?"

"You scientific men are always so severe. And it really is extraordinary the way one seems to positively know things sometimes—just know them, feel them, I mean—quite uncanny—it really is. Claire knows what I mean, don't you, Claire?"

She appealed to her hostess with a slight pout, and a tilted shoulder.

Claire Trent did not reply at once. It was a small dinner party—she and her husband, Violet Eversleigh, Sir Alington West, and his nephew Dermot West, who was an old friend of Jack Trent's. Jack Trent himself, a somewhat heavy, florid man with a good-humored smile and a pleasant lazy laugh, took up the thread.

"Bunkum, Violet! Your best friend is killed in a railway accident. Straight away you remember that you dreamed of a black cat last Tuesday—marvelous, you felt all along that something was going to happen!"

"Oh, no, Jack, you're mixing up premonitions with intuition now. Come, now, Sir Alington, you must admit that premonitions are real?"

"To a certain extent, perhaps," admitted the physician cautiously. "But coincidence accounts for a good deal, and then there is the invariable tendency to make the most of a story afterward."

"I don't think there is any such thing as premonition," said Claire Trent rather abruptly. "Or intuition or a sixth sense or any of the things we talk about so glibly. We go through life like a train rushing through the darkness to an unknown destination."

"That's hardly a good simile, Mrs. Trent," said Dermot West, lifting his head for the first time and taking part in the discussion. There was a curious glitter in the clear gray eyes that shone out rather oddly from the deeply tanned face. "You've forgotten the signals, you see."

"The signals?"

"Yes, green if it's all right, and red—for danger!"

"Red—for danger—how thrilling!" breathed Violet Eversleigh.

Dermot turned from her rather impatiently. "That's just a way of describing it, of course."

Trent stared at him curiously. "You speak as though it were an actual experience, Dermot, old boy."

"So it is—has been, I mean."

"Give us the yarn."

"I can give you one instance. Out in Mesopotamia, just after the Armistice, I came into my tent one evening with the feeling strong upon me. Danger! Look out! Hadn't the ghost of a notion what it was all about. I made a round of the camp, fussed unnecessarily, took all precautions against an attack by hostile Arabs. Then I went back to my tent. As soon as I got inside, the feeling popped up again stronger than ever. Danger! In the end I took a blanket outside, rolled myself up in it, and slept there."

"Well?"

"The next morning, when I went inside the tent, first thing I saw was a great knife arrangement—about half a yard long—struck down through my bunk, just where I would have lain. I soon found out about it—one of the Arab servants. His son had been shot as a spy. What have you got to say to that, Uncle Alington, as an example of what I call the red signal?"

The specialist smiled noncommittally. "A very interesting story, my dear Dermot."

"But not one that you accept unreservedly?"

"Yes, yes, I have no doubt but that you had the premonition of danger, just as you state. But it is the origin of the premonition I dispute. According to you, it came from without, impressed by some outside source upon your mentality. But nowadays we find that nearly everything comes from within—from our subconscious self.

"I suggest that by some glance or look this Arab had betrayed himself. Your conscious self did not notice or remember, but with your subconscious self it was otherwise. The subconscious never forgets. We believe, too, that it can reason and deduce quite independently of the higher or conscious will. Your subconscious self, then, believed that an attempt might be made to assassinate you, and succeeded in forcing its fear upon your conscious realization."

"That sounds very convincing, I admit," said Dermot, smiling.

"But not nearly so exciting," pouted Mrs. Eversleigh.

"It is also possible that you may have been subconsciously aware of the hate felt by the man toward you. What in old days used to be called telepathy certainly exists, though the conditions governing it are very little understood."

"Have there been any other instances?" asked Claire of Dermot.

"Oh! yes, but nothing very pictorial—and I suppose they could all be explained under the heading of coincidence. I refused an invitation to a country house once, for no other reason than the 'red signal.' The place was burned out during the week. By the way, Uncle Alington, where does the subconscious come in there?"

"I'm afraid it doesn't," said Sir Alington, smiling.

"But you've got an equally good explanation. Come, now. No need to be tactful with near relatives."

"Well, then, nephew, I venture to suggest that you refused the invitation for the ordinary reason that you didn't much want to go, and that after the fire, you suggested to yourself that you had had a warning of danger, which explanation you now believe implicitly."

"It's hopeless," laughed Dermot. "It's heads you win, tails I lose."

"Never mind, Mr. West," cried Violet Eversleigh. "I believe in your Red Signal. Is the time in Mesopotamia the last time you had it?"

"Yes—until—"

"I beg your pardon?"

"Nothing."

Dermot sat silent. The words which had nearly left his lips were: "Yes, until tonight." They had come quite unbidden to his lips, voicing a thought which had as yet not been consciously realized, but he was aware at once that they were true. The Red Signal was looming up out of the darkness. Danger! Danger close at hand!

But why? What conceivable danger could there be here? Here in the house of his friends? At least—well, yes, there was that kind of danger. He looked at Claire Trent—her whiteness, her slenderness, the exquisite droop of her golden head. But that danger had been there for some time —it was never likely to get acute. For Jack Trent was his best friend, and more than his best friend, the man who had saved his life in Flanders and been recommended for the V.C. for doing so. A good fellow, Jack, one of the best. Damned bad luck that he should have fallen in love with Jack's wife. He'd get over it some day, he supposed. A thing couldn't go on hurting like this forever. One could starve it out—that was it, starve it out. It was not as though she would ever guess—and if she did guess, there was no danger of her caring. A statue, a beautiful statue, a thing of gold and ivory and pale-pink coral—a toy for a king, not a real woman.

Claire—the very thought of her name, uttered silently, hurt him. He must get over it. He'd cared for women before. *But not like this!* said something. *Not like this.* Well, there it was. No danger there—heartache, yes, but not danger. Not the danger of the Red Signal. That was for something else.

He looked round the table and it struck him for the first time that it was rather an unusual little gathering. His uncle, for instance, seldom dined out in this small, informal way. It was not as though the Trents were old friends; until this evening Dermot had not been aware that he knew them at all.

To be sure, there was an excuse. A rather notorious medium was coming after dinner to give a séance. Sir Alington professed to be mildly interested in spiritualism. Yes, that was an excuse, certainly.

The word forced itself on his notice. An excuse. Was the séance just an excuse to make the specialist's presence at dinner natural? If so, what was the real object of his being here? A host of details came rushing into Dermot's mind, trifles unnoticed at the time, or, as his uncle would have said, unnoticed by the conscious mind.

The great physician had looked oddly, very oddly, at Claire more than once. He seemed to be watching her. She was uneasy under his scrutiny. She made little twitching motions with her hands. She was nervous, horribly nervous, and was it, could it be, frightened? Why was she frightened?

With a jerk he came back to the conversation round the table. Mrs. Eversleigh had got the great man talking upon his own subject.

"My dear lady," he was saying, "what *is* madness? I can assure you that the more we study the subject, the more difficult we find it to pronounce. We all practice a certain amount of self-deception, and when we carry it so far as to believe we are the Czar of Russia, we are shut up or restrained. But there is a long road before we reach that point. At what particular spot on it shall we erect a post and say, 'On this side sanity, on the other madness'? It can't be done, you know. And I will tell you this—if the man suffering from a delusion happened to hold his tongue about it, in all probability we should never be able to distinguish him from a normal individual. The extraordinary sanity of the insane is an interesting subject."

Sir Alington sipped his wine with appreciation and beamed upon the company.

"I've always heard they are very cunning," remarked Mrs. Eversleigh. "Loonies, I mean."

"Remarkably so. And suppression of one's particular delusion has a disastrous effect very often. All suppressions are dangerous, as psychoanalysis has taught us. The man who has a harmless eccentricity, and can indulge it as such, seldom goes over the border line. But the man—" he paused—"or woman who is to all appearance perfectly normal, may be in reality a poignant source of danger to the community."

His gaze traveled gently down the table to Claire and then back again.

A horrible fear shook Dermot. Was that what he meant? Was that what he was driving at? Impossible, but—

"And all from suppressing oneself," sighed Mrs. Eversleigh. "I quite see that one should be very careful always to—to express one's personality. The dangers of the other are frightful."

"My dear Mrs. Eversleigh," expostulated the physician, "you have quite misunderstood me. The cause of the mischief is in the physical matter of the brain—sometimes arising from some outward agency such as a blow, sometimes, alas, congenital."

"Heredity is so sad," sighed the lady vaguely. "Consumption and all that."

"Tuberculosis is not hereditary," said Sir Alington dryly.

"Isn't it? I always thought it was. But madness is! How dreadful. What else?"

"Gout," said Sir Alington, smiling. "And color blindness —the latter is rather interesting. It is transmitted direct to males, but is latent in females. So while there are many color-blind men, for a woman to be color blind, it must have been latent in her mother as well as present in her father—rather an unusual state of things to occur. That is what is called sex-limited heredity."

"How interesting. But madness is not like that, is it?"

"Madness can be handed down to men or women equally," said the physician gravely.

Claire rose suddenly, pushing back her chair so abruptly that it overturned and fell to the ground. She was very pale, and the nervous motions of her fingers were very apparent.

"You—you will not be long, will you?" she begged. "Mrs. Thompson will be here in a few minutes now."

"One glass of port and I will be with you," declared Sir Alington. "To see this wonderful Mrs. Thompson's performance is what I have come for, is it not? Ha, ha! Not that I needed any inducement." He bowed.

Claire gave a faint smile of acknowledgment and passed out of the room with Mrs. Eversleigh.

"Afraid I've been talking shop," remarked the physician as he resumed his seat. "Forgive me, my dear fellow."

"Not at all," said Trent perfunctorily.

He looked strained and worried. For the first time Dermot felt an outsider in the company of his friend. Between these two was a secret that even an old friend might not share. And yet the whole thing was fantastic and incredible. What had he to go upon? Nothing but a couple of glances and a woman's nervousness.

They lingered over their wine but a very short time, and arrived up in the drawing-room just as Mrs. Thompson was announced.

The medium was a plump middle-aged woman, atrociously dressed in magenta velvet, with a loud, rather common voice.

"Hope I'm not late, Mrs. Trent," she said cheerily. "You did say nine o'clock, didn't you?"

"You are quite punctual, Mrs. Thompson," said Claire in her sweet, slightly husky voice. "This is our little circle."

No further introductions were made, as was evidently the custom. The medium swept them all with a shrewd, penetrating eye.

"I hope we shall get some good results," she remarked briskly. "I can't tell you how I hate it when I go out and I can't give satisfaction, so to speak. It just makes me mad. But I think Shiromako—my Japanese control, you know— will be able to get through all right tonight. I'm feeling ever so fit, and I refused the Welsh rarebit, fond of cheese though I am."

Dermot listened, half-amused, half-disgusted. How prosaic the whole thing was! And yet, was he not judging foolishly? Everything, after all, was natural—the powers claimed by mediums were natural powers, as yet imperfectly understood. A great surgeon might be wary of indigestion on the eve of a delicate operation. Why not Mrs. Thompson?

Chairs were arranged in a circle, lights so that they could conveniently be raised and lowered. Dermot noticed that there was no question of tests, or of Sir Alington satisfying himself as to the conditions of the séance. No, this business of Mrs. Thompson was only a blind. Sir Alington was here for quite another purpose. Claire's mother, Dermot remembered, had died abroad. There had been some mystery about her— Hereditary—

With a jerk he forced his mind back to the surroundings of the moment.

Everyone took their places, and the lights were turned out, all but a small red-shaded one on a far table.

For a while nothing was heard but the low, even breathing of the medium. Gradually it grew more and more stertorous. Then, with a suddenness that made Dermot jump, a loud rap came from the far end of the room. It was repeated from the other side. Then a perfect crescendo of raps was heard. They died away, and a sudden high peal of mocking laughter rang through the room.

Then silence, broken by a voice utterly unlike that of Mrs. Thompson, a high-pitched, quaintly inflected voice.

"I am here, gentlemen," it said. "Yess, I am here. You wish to ask me things?"

"Who are you? Shiromako?"

"Yess. I Shiromako. I pass over long ago. I work. I very happy."

Further details of Shiromako's life followed. It was all very flat and uninteresting, and Dermot had heard it often before. Everyone was happy, very happy. Messages were given from vaguely described relatives, the description being so loosely worded as to fit almost any contingency. An elderly lady, the mother of someone present, held the floor for some time, imparting copybook maxims with an air of refreshing novelty hardly borne out by her subject matter.

"Someone else want to get through now," announced Shiromako. "Got a very important message for one of the gentlemen."

There was a pause, and then a new voice spoke, prefacing its remarks with an evil, demoniacal chuckle.

"Ha, ha! Ha, ha, ha! Better not go home. Take my advice."

"Who are you speaking to?" asked Trent.

"One of you three. I shouldn't go home if I were him. Danger! Blood! Not very much blood—quite enough. No, don't go home." The voice grew fainter. *"Don't go home!"*

It died away completely. Dermot felt his blood tingling. He was convinced that the warning was meant for him. Somehow or other, there was danger abroad tonight.

There was a sigh from the medium, and then a groan. She was coming round. The lights were turned on, and presently she sat upright, her eyes blinking a little.

"Go off well, my dear? I hope so."

"Very good indeed, thank you, Mrs. Thompson."

"Shiromako, I suppose?"

"Yes, and others."

Mrs. Thompson yawned.

"I'm dead beat. Absolutely down and out. Does fairly take it out of you. Well, I'm glad it was a success. I was a bit afraid something disagreeable might happen. There's a queer feel about this room tonight."

She glanced over each ample shoulder in turn, and then shrugged them uncomfortably.

"I don't like it," she said. "Any sudden deaths among any of you people lately?"

"What do you mean—among us?"

"Near relatives—dear friends? No? Well, if I wanted to be melodramatic, I'd say that there was death in the air tonight. There, it's only my nonsense. Good-by, Mrs. Trent. I'm glad you've been satisfied."

Mrs. Thompson in her magenta velvet gown went out.

"I hope you've been interested, Sir Alington," murmured Claire.

"A most interesting evening, my dear lady. Many thanks for the opportunity. Let me wish you good night. You are all going on to a dance, are you not?"

"Won't you come with us?"

"No, no. I make it a rule to be in bed by half past eleven. Good night. Good night, Mrs. Eversleigh. Ah, Dermot, I rather want to have a word with you. Can you come with me now? You can rejoin the others at the Grafton Galleries."

"Certainly, Uncle. I'll meet you there, then, Trent."

Very few words were exchanged between uncle and nephew during the short drive to Harley Street. Sir Alington made a semi-apology for dragging Dermot away, and assured him that he would only detain him a few minutes.

"Shall I keep the car for you, my boy?" he asked, as they alighted.

"Oh, don't bother, Uncle. I'll pick up a taxi."

"Very good. I don't like to keep Charlson up later than I can help. Good night, Charlson. Now where the devil did I put my key?"

The car glided away as Sir Alington stood on the steps searching his pockets.

"Must have left it in my other coat," he said at length. "Ring the bell, will you? Johnson is still up, I dare say."

The imperturbable Johnson did indeed open the door within sixty seconds.

"Mislaid my key, Johnson," explained Sir Alington. "Bring a couple of whiskies and sodas into the library."

"Very good, Sir Alington."

The physician strode on into the library and turned on the lights. He motioned to Dermot to close the door.

"I won't keep you long, Dermot, but there's just something I want to say to you. Is it my fancy, or have you a certain—*tendresse,* shall we say, for Mrs. Jack Trent?"

The blood rushed to Dermot's face.

"Jack Trent is my best friend."

"Pardon me, but that is hardly answering my question. I dare say that you consider my views on divorce and such matters highly puritanical, but I must remind you that you are my only near relative and my heir."

"There is no question of a divorce," said Dermot angrily.

"There certainly is not, for a reason which I understand

perhaps better than you do. That particular reason I cannot give you now, but I do wish to warn you. She is not for you."

The young man faced his uncle's gaze steadily. "I do understand—and permit me to say, perhaps better than you think. I know the reason for your presence at dinner tonight."

"Eh?" The physician was clearly startled. "How did you know that?"

"Call it a guess, sir. I am right, am I not, when I say that you were there in your—professional capacity."

Sir Alington strode up and down.

"You are quite right, Dermot. I could not, of course, have told you so myself, though I am afraid it will soon be common property."

Dermot's heart contracted. "You mean that you have —made up your mind?"

"Yes, there is insanity in the family—on the mother's side. A sad case—a very sad case."

"I can't believe it, sir."

"I dare say not. To the layman there are few if any signs apparent."

"And to the expert?"

"The evidence is conclusive. In such a case the patient must be placed under restraint as soon as possible."

"My God!" breathed Dermot. "But you can't shut anyone up for nothing at all."

"My dear Dermot! Cases are only placed under restraint when their being at large would result in danger to the community."

"Danger?"

"Very grave danger. In all probability a peculiar form of homicidal mania. It was so in the mother's case."

Dermot turned away with a groan, burying his face in his hands. Claire—white and golden Claire!

"In the circumstances," continued the physician comfortably, "I felt it incumbent on me to warn you."

"Claire," murmured Dermot. "My poor Claire."

"Yes, indeed, we must all pity her."

Suddenly Dermot raised his head.

"I say I don't believe it. Doctors make mistakes. Everyone knows that. And they're always keen on their own specialty."

"My dear Dermot," cried Sir Alington angrily.

"I tell you I don't believe it—and anyway, even if it is so, I don't care. I love Claire. If she will come with me, I shall take her away—far away—out of the reach of meddling physicians. I shall guard her, care for her, shelter her with my love."

"You will do nothing of the sort. Are you mad?"

Dermot laughed scornfully. "*You* would say so."

"Understand me, Dermot." Sir Alington's face was red with suppressed passion. "If you do this thing—this shameful thing—I shall withdraw the allowance I am now making you, and I shall make a new will leaving all I possess to various hospitals."

"Do as you please with your damned money," said Dermot in a low voice. "I shall have the woman I love."

"A woman who—"

"Say a word against her and, by God, I'll kill you!" cried Dermot.

A slight chink of glasses made them both swing round. Unheard by them in the heat of their argument, Johnson had entered with a tray of glasses. His face was the imperturbable one of the good servant, but Dermot wondered just exactly how much he had overheard.

"That'll do, Johnson," said Sir Alington curtly. "You can go to bed."

"Thank you, sir. Good night, sir."

Johnson withdrew.

The two men looked at each other. The momentary interruption had calmed the storm.

"Uncle," said Dermot. "I shouldn't have spoken to you as I did. I can quite see that from your point of view you are perfectly right. But I have loved Claire Trent for a long time. The fact that Jack Trent is my best friend has hitherto stood in the way of my ever speaking of love to Claire herself. But in these circumstances that fact no longer counts. The idea that any monetary conditions can deter me is absurd. I think we've both said all there is to be said. Good night."

"Dermot—"

"It is really no good arguing further. Good night, Uncle Alington."

He went out quickly, shutting the door behind him. The hall was in darkness. He passed through it, opened the front door and emerged into the street, banging the door behind him.

A taxi had just deposited a fare at a house farther along the street and Dermot hailed it, and drove to the Grafton Galleries.

In the door of the ballroom he stood for a minute, bewildered, his head spinning. The raucous jazz music, the smiling women—it was as though he had stepped into another world.

Had he dreamed it all? Impossible that that grim conversation with his uncle should have really taken place. There was Claire floating past, like a lily in her white-and-silver gown that fitted sheathlike to her slenderness. She smiled at him, her face calm and serene. Surely it was all a dream.

The dance had stopped. Presently she was near him, smiling up into his face. As in a dream he asked her to dance. She was in his arms now, the raucous melodies had begun again.

He felt her flag a little.

"Tired? Do you want to stop?"

"If you don't mind. Can we go somewhere where we can

talk? There is something I want to say to you."

Not a dream. He came back to earth with a bump. Could he ever have thought her face calm and serene? It was haunted with anxiety, with dread. How much did she know?

He found a quiet corner, and they sat down side by side.

"Well," he said, assuming a lightness he did not feel, "you said you had something you wanted to say to me?"

"Yes." Her eyes were cast down. She was playing nervously with the tassel of her gown. "It's difficult—"

"Tell me, Claire."

"It's just this. I want you to—to go away for a time."

He was astonished. Whatever he had expected, it was not this.

"You want me to go away? Why?"

"It's best to be honest, isn't it? I know that you are a—a gentleman and my friend. I want you to go away because I—I have let myself get fond of you."

"Claire."

Her words left him dumb—tongue-tied.

"Please do not think that I am conceited enough to fancy that you—would ever be likely to fall in love with me. It is only that—I am not very happy—and—oh! I would rather you went away."

"Claire, don't you know that I have cared—cared damnably—ever since I met you?"

She lifted startled eyes to his face.

"You cared? You have cared a long time?"

"Since the beginning."

"Oh!" she cried. "Why didn't you tell me? Then! When I could have come to you! Why tell me now when it's too late. No, I'm mad—I don't know what I'm saying. I could never have come to you."

"Claire, what did you mean when you said 'now that it's too late'? Is it—is it because of my uncle? What he knows?"

She nodded, the tears running down her face.

"Listen, Claire, you're not to believe all that. You're not to think about it. Instead, you will come away with me. I will look after you—keep you safe always."

His arms went round her. He drew her to him, felt her tremble at his touch. Then suddenly she wrenched herself free.

"Oh, no, please. Can't you see? I couldn't now. It would be ugly—ugly—ugly. All along I've wanted to be good—and now—it would be ugly as well."

He hesitated, baffled by her words. She looked at him appealingly.

"Please," she said. "I want to be good."

Without a word, Dermot got up and left her. For the moment he was touched and racked by her words beyond argument. He went for his hat and coat, running into Trent as he did so.

"Hallo, Dermot, you're off early."

"Yes, I'm not in the mood for dancing tonight."

"It's a rotten night," said Trent gloomily. "But you haven't got my worries."

Dermot had a sudden panic that Trent might be going to confide in him. Not that—anything but that!

"Well, so long," he said hurriedly. "I'm off home."

"Home, eh? What about the warning of the spirits?"

"I'll risk that. Good night, Jack."

Dermot's flat was not far away. He walked there, feeling the need of the cool night air to calm his fevered brain. He let himself in with his key and switched on the light in the bedroom.

And all at once, for the second time that night, the feeling of the Red Signal surged over him. So overpowering was it that for the moment it swept even Claire from his mind.

Danger! He was in danger. At this very moment, in this very room!

He tried in vain to ridicule himself free of the fear. Perhaps his efforts were secretly halfhearted. So far, the Red Signal had given him timely warning which had enabled him to avoid disaster. Smiling a little at his own superstition, he made a careful tour of the flat. It was possible that some malefactor had got in and was lying concealed there. But his search revealed nothing. His man, Milson, was away, and the flat was absolutely empty.

He returned to his bedroom and undressed slowly, frowning to himself. The sense of danger was acute as ever. He went to a drawer to get out a handkerchief, and suddenly stood stock still. There was an unfamiliar lump in the middle of the drawer.

His quick nervous fingers tore aside the handkerchiefs and took out the object concealed beneath them.

It was a revolver.

With the utmost astonishment Dermot examined it keenly. It was of a somewhat unfamiliar pattern, and one shot had been fired from it lately. Beyond that he could make nothing of it. Someone had placed it in that drawer that very evening. It had not been there when he dressed for dinner—he was sure of that.

He was about to replace it in the drawer, when he was startled by a bell ringing. It rang again and again, sounding unusually loud in the quietness of the empty flat.

Who could be coming to the front door at this hour? And only one answer came to the question—an answer instinctive and persistent.

Danger—danger—danger.

Led by some instinct for which he did not account, Dermot switched off his light, slipped on an overcoat that lay across a chair, and opened the hall door.

Two men stood outside. Beyond them Dermot caught sight of a blue uniform. A policeman!

"Mr. West?" asked one of the two men.

It seemed to Dermot that ages elapsed before he answered. In reality it was only a few seconds before he replied in a very fair imitation of his servant's expressionless voice, "Mr. West hasn't come in yet."

"Hasn't come in yet, eh? Very well, then, I think we'd better come in and wait for him."

"No, you don't."

"See here, my man, I'm Inspector Verall of Scotland Yard, and I've got a warrant for the arrest of your master. You can see it if you like."

Dermot perused the proffered paper, or pretended to do so, asking in a dazed voice, "What for? What's he done?"

"Murder. Sir Alington West of Harley Street."

His brain in a whirl, Dermot fell back before his redoubtable visitors. He went into the sitting-room and switched on the light. The inspector followed him.

"Have a search round," he directed the other man. Then he turned to Dermot. "You stay here, my man. No slipping off to warn your master. What's your name, by the way?"

"Milson, sir."

"What time do you expect your master in, Milson?"

"I don't know, sir, he was going to a dance, I believe. At the Grafton Galleries."

"He left there just under an hour ago. Sure he's not been back here?"

"I don't think so, sir. I fancy I should have heard him come in."

At this moment the second man came in from the adjoining room. In his hand he carried the revolver. He took it across to the inspector in some excitement. An expression of satisfaction flitted across the latter's face.

"That settles it," he remarked. "Must have slipped in and out without your hearing him. He's hooked it by now. I'd better be off. Cawley, you stay here, in case he should come back again, and you can keep an eye on this fellow. He may know more about his master than he pretends."

The inspector bustled off. Dermot endeavored to get the

details of the affair from Cawley, who was quite ready to be talkative.

"Pretty clear case," he vouchsafed. "The murder was discovered almost immediately. Johnson, the manservant, had only just gone up to bed when he fancied he heard a shot, and came down again. Found Sir Alington dead, shot through the heart. He rang us up at once and we came along and heard his story."

"Which made it a pretty clear case?" ventured Dermot.

"Absolutely. This young West came in with his uncle and they were quarreling when Johnson brought in the drinks. The old boy was threatening to make a new will, and your master was talking about shooting him. Not five minutes later the shot was heard. Oh, yes, clear enough."

Clear enough indeed. Dermot's heart sank as he realized the overwhelming evidence against him. And no way out save flight. He set his wits to work. Presently he suggested making a cup of tea. Cawley assented readily enough. He had already searched the flat and knew there was no back entrance.

Dermot was permitted to depart to the kitchen. Once there he put the kettle on, and chinked cups and saucers industriously. Then he stole swiftly to the window and lifted the sash. The flat was on the second floor, and outside the window was the small wire lift used by tradesmen which ran up and down on its steel cable.

Like a flash Dermot was outside the window and swinging himself down the wire rope. It cut into his hands, making them bleed, but he went on desperately.

A few minutes later he was emerging cautiously from the back of the block. Turning the corner, he cannoned into a figure standing by the sidewalk. To his utter amazement he recognized Jack Trent. Trent was fully alive to the perils of the situation.

"My God! Dermot! Quick, don't hang about here."

Taking him by the arm, he led him down a by street,

then down another. A lonely taxi was sighted and hailed and they jumped in, Trent giving the man his own address.

"Safest place for the moment. There we can decide what to do next to put those fools off the track. I came round here, hoping to be able to warn you before the police got here."

"I didn't even know that you had heard of it. Jack, you don't believe—"

"Of course not, old fellow, not for one minute. I know you far too well. All the same, it's a nasty business for you. They came round asking questions—what time you got to the Grafton Galleries, when you left, and so on. Dermot, who could have done the old boy in?"

"I can't imagine. Whoever did it put the revolver in my drawer, I suppose. Must have been watching us pretty closely."

"That séance business was damned funny. 'Don't go home.' Meant for poor old West. He did go home, and got shot."

"It applies to me, too," said Dermot. "I went home and found a planted revolver and a police inspector."

"Well, I hope it doesn't get me, too," said Trent. "Here we are."

He paid the taxi, opened the door with his latchkey, and guided Dermot up the dark stairs to his den, a small room on the first floor.

He threw open the door and Dermot walked in, while Trent switched on the light, and came to join him.

"Pretty safe here for the time being," he remarked. "Now we can get our heads together and decide what is best to be done."

"I've made a fool of myself," said Dermot suddenly. "I ought to have faced it out. I see more clearly now. The whole thing's a plot. What the devil are you laughing at?"

For Trent was leaning back in his chair, shaking with

unrestrained mirth. There was something horrible in the sound—something horrible, too, about the man altogether. There was a curious light in his eyes.

"A damned clever plot," he gasped out. "Dermot, you're done for."

He drew the telephone toward him.

"What are you going to do?" asked Dermot.

"Ring up Scotland Yard. Tell 'em their bird's here—safe under lock and key. Yes, I locked the door when I came in and the key's in my pocket. No good looking at that other door behind me. That leads into Claire's room, and she always locks it on her side. She's afraid of me, you know. Been afraid of me a long time. She always knows when I'm thinking about that knife—a long, sharp knife. No, you don't—"

Dermot had been about to make a rush at him, but the other had suddenly produced a revolver.

"That's the second of them," chuckled Trent. "I put the first in your drawer—after shooting old West with it— What are you looking at over my head? That door? It's no use, even if Claire were to open it—and she might to you—I'd shoot you before you got there. Not in the heart—not to kill, just wing you, so that you couldn't get away. I'm a jolly good shot, you know. I saved your life once. More fool I. No, no, I want you hanged—yes, hanged. It isn't you I want the knife for. It's Claire—pretty Claire, so white and soft. Old West knew. That's what he was here for tonight, to see if I were mad or not. He wanted to shut me up—so that I shouldn't get at Claire with a knife. I was very cunning. I took his latchkey and yours, too. I slipped away from the dance as soon as I got there. I saw you come out of his house, and I went in. I shot him and came away at once. Then I went to your place and left the revolver. I was at the Grafton Galleries again almost as soon as you were, and I put the latchkey back in your coat pocket when I was saying good night to you. I don't mind telling you all this. There's no one else to hear, and when you're being hanged I'd like you to know I did it. There's not a loophole of escape. It makes me laugh— God, how it makes me laugh! What are you thinking of? What the devil are you looking at?"

"I'm thinking of some words you quoted just now. You'd have done better, Trent, not to come home."

"What do you mean?"

"Look behind you."

Trent spun round. In the doorway of the communicating room stood Claire—and Inspector Verall.

Trent was quick. The revolver spoke just once—and found its mark. He fell forward across the table. The inspector sprang to his side, as Dermot stared at Claire in a dream. Thoughts flashed through his brain disjointedly. His uncle—their quarrel—the colossal misunderstanding —the divorce laws of England which would never free Claire from an insane husband—"we must all pity her"— the plot between her and Sir Alington which the cunning of Trent had seen through—her cry to him, "Ugly—ugly— ugly!" Yes, but now—

The inspector straightened up.

"Dead," he said vexedly.

"Yes," Dermot heard himself saying, "he was always a good shot."

THE FOURTH MAN

CANON PARFITT PANTED A LITTLE. Running for trains was not much of a business for a man of his age. For one thing his figure was not what it was and with the loss of his slender silhouette went an increasing tendency to be short of breath. This tendency the Canon himself always referred to, with dignity, as "My heart, you know!"

He sank into the corner of the first-class carriage with a sigh of relief. The warmth of the heated carriage was most agreeable to him. Outside the snow was falling. Lucky to get a corner seat on a long night journey. Miserable business if you didn't. There ought to be a sleeper on this train.

The other three corners were already occupied, and noting this fact Canon Parfitt became aware that the man in the far corner was smiling at him in gentle recognition. He was a clean-shaven man with a quizzical face and hair just turning gray on the temples. His profession was so clearly the law that no one could have mistaken him for anything else for a moment. Sir George Durand was, indeed, a very famous lawyer.

"Well, Parfitt," he remarked genially, "you had a run for it, didn't you?"

"Very bad for my heart, I'm afraid," said the Canon. "Quite a coincidence meeting you, Sir George. Are you going far north?"

"Newcastle," said Sir George laconically. "By the way," he added, "do you know Doctor Campbell Clark?"

The man sitting on the same side of the carriage as the Canon inclined his head pleasantly.

"We met on the platform," continued the lawyer. "Another coincidence."

Canon Parfitt looked at Dr. Campbell Clark with a good deal of interest. It was a name of which he had often heard. Dr. Clark was in the forefront as a physician and mental specialist, and his last book, *The Problem of the Unconscious Mind,* had been the most discussed book of the year.

Canon Parfitt saw a square jaw, very steady blue eyes, and reddish hair untouched by gray, but thinning rapidly. And he received also the impression of a very forceful personality.

By a perfectly natural association of ideas the Canon looked across to the seat opposite him, half-expecting to receive a glance of recognition there also, but the fourth occupant of the carriage proved to be a total stranger—a foreigner, the Canon fancied. He was a slight, dark man, rather insignificant in appearance. Hunched in a big overcoat, he appeared to be fast asleep.

"Canon Parfitt of Bradchester?" inquired Dr. Campbell Clark in a pleasant voice.

The Canon looked flattered. Those "scientific sermons" of his had really made a great hit—especially since the press had taken them up. Well, that was what the Church needed—good modern up-to-date stuff.

"I have read your book with great interest, Doctor Campbell Clark," he said. "Though it's a bit too technical here and there for me to follow."

Durand broke in. "Are you for talking or sleeping, Canon?" he asked. "I'll confess at once that I suffer from insomnia and that therefore I'm in favor of the former."

"Oh, certainly! By all means," said the Canon. "I seldom sleep on these night journeys and the book I have with me is a very dull one."

"We are at any rate a representative gathering," remarked the doctor with a smile. "The Church, the law, the medical profession."

"Not much we couldn't give an opinion on between us,

eh?" laughed Durand. "The Church for the spiritual view, myself for the purely worldly and legal view, and you, doctor, with the widest field of all, ranging from the purely pathological to the—super-psychological! Among the three of us we should cover any ground pretty completely, I fancy."

"Not so completely as you imagine, I think," said Dr. Clark. "There's another point of view, you know, that you left out, and that's rather an important one."

"Meaning?" queried the lawyer.

"The point of view of the man in the street."

"Is that so important? Isn't the man in the street usually wrong?"

"Oh, almost always! But he has the thing that all expert opinion must lack—the personal point of view. In the end, you know, you can't get away from personal relationships. I've found that in my profession. For every patient who comes to me genuinely ill, at least five come who have nothing whatever the matter with them except an inability to live happily with the inmates of the same house. They call it everything—from housemaid's knee to writer's cramp, but it's all the same thing, the raw surface produced by mind rubbing against mind."

"You have a lot of patients with 'nerves,' I suppose," the Canon remarked disparagingly. His own nerves were excellent.

"Ah, and what do you mean by that?" The other swung round on him, quick as a flash. "Nerves! People use that word and laugh after it, just as you did. 'Nothing the matter with so and so,' they say. 'Just nerves.' But, good God, man, you've got the crux of everything there! You can get at a mere bodily ailment and heal it. But at this day we know very little more about the obscure causes of the hundred and one forms of nervous disease than we did in—well, the reign of Queen Elizabeth!"

"Dear me," said Canon Parfitt, a little bewildered

by this onslaught. "Is that so?"

"Mind you, it's a sign of grace," Dr. Campbell Clark went on. "In the old days we considered man a simple animal, body and soul—with stress laid on the former."

"Body, soul, and spirit," corrected the clergyman mildly.

"Spirit?" The doctor smiled oddly. "What do you parsons mean exactly by spirit? You've never been very clear about it, you know. All down the ages you've funked an exact definition."

The Canon cleared his throat in preparation for speech, but to his chagrin he was given no opportunity. The doctor went on. "Are we even sure the word is spirit—might it not be spirits?"

"Spirits?" Sir George Durand questioned, his eyebrows raised quizzically.

"Yes." Campbell Clark's gaze transferred itself to him. He leaned forward and tapped the other man lightly on the breast. "Are you so sure," he said gravely, "that there is only one occupant of this structure—for that is all it is, you know—this desirable residence to be let furnished—for seven, twenty-one, forty-one, seventy-one—whatever it may be!—years? And in the end the tenant moves his things out—little by little—and then goes out of the house altogether—and down comes the house, a mass of ruin and decay. You're the master of the house, we'll admit that, but aren't you ever conscious of the presence of others—soft-footed servants, hardly noticed, except for the work they do—work that you're not conscious of having done? Or friends—moods that take hold of you and make you, for the time being, a 'different man,' as the saying goes? You're the king of the castle, right enough, but be very sure the 'dirty rascal' is there, too."

"My dear Clark," drawled the lawyer, "you make me positively uncomfortable. Is my mind really a battleground of conflicting personalities? Is that science's latest?"

It was the doctor's turn to shrug his shoulders. "Your

body is," he said dryly. "If the body, why not the mind?"

"Very interesting," said Canon Parfitt. "Ah! Wonderful science—wonderful science."

And inwardly he thought to himself: *I can get a most arresting sermon out of the idea.*

But Dr. Campbell Clark had leaned back again in his seat, his momentary excitement spent.

"As a matter of fact," he remarked in a dry, professional manner, "it is a case of dual personality that takes me to Newcastle tonight. Very interesting case. Neurotic subject, of course. But quite genuine."

"Dual personality," said Sir George Durand thoughtfully. "It's not so very rare, I believe. There's loss of memory as well, isn't there? I know the matter cropped up in a case in the Probate Court the other day."

Dr. Clark nodded.

"The classic case, of course," he said, "was that of Felicie Bault. You may remember hearing of it?"

"Of course," said Canon Parfitt. "I remember reading about it in the papers—but quite a long time ago—seven years at least."

Dr. Campbell Clark nodded.

"That girl became one of the most famous figures in France. Scientists from all over the world came to see her. She had no less than four distinct personalities. They were known as Felicie One, Felicie Two, Felicie Three, etc."

"Wasn't there some suggestion of deliberate trickery?" asked Sir George alertly.

"The personalities of Felicie Three and Felicie Four were a little open to doubt," admitted the doctor. "But the main facts remain. Felicie Bault was a Brittany peasant girl. She was the third of a family of five, the daughter of a drunken father and a mentally defective mother. In one of his drinking bouts the father strangled the mother and was, if I remember rightly, transported for life. Felicie was then five years of age. Some charitable people interested themselves in the children and Felicie was brought up and educated by an English maiden lady who had a kind of home for destitute children. She could make very little of Felicie, however. She describes the girl as abnormally slow and stupid, taught to read and write only with the greatest difficulty, and clumsy with her hands. This lady, Miss Slater, tried to fit the girl for domestic service, and did indeed find her several places when she was of an age to take them. But she never stayed long anywhere owing to her stupidity and also her intense laziness."

The doctor paused for a minute, and the Canon, recrossing his legs and arranging his traveling rug more closely round him, was suddenly aware that the man opposite him had moved very slightly. His eyes, which had formerly been shut, were now open, and something in them, something mocking and indefinable, startled the worthy Canon. It was as though the man were listening and gloating secretly over what he heard.

"There is a photograph taken of Felicie Bault at the age of seventeen," continued the doctor. "It shows her as a loutish peasant girl, heavy of build. There is nothing in that picture to indicate that she was soon to be one of the most famous persons in France.

"Five years later, when she was 22, Felicie Bault had a severe nervous illness, and on recovery the strange phenomena began to manifest themselves. The following are facts attested to by many eminent scientists. The personality called Felicie One was indistinguishable from the Felicie Bault of the last twenty-two years. Felicie One wrote French badly and haltingly, spoke no foreign languages, and was unable to play the piano. Felicie Two, on the contrary, spoke Italian fluently and German moderately. Her handwriting was quite different from that of Felicie One, and she wrote fluent and expressive French. She could discuss politics and art and she was passionately fond of playing the piano. Felicie Three had many points in common with Felicie Two. She was intelligent and apparently well educated, but in moral character she was a total contrast. She appeared, in fact, an utterly depraved creature—but depraved in a Parisian and not a provincial way. She knew all the Paris *argot,* and the expressions of the chic *demi monde.* Her language was filthy and she would rail against religion and so-called 'good people' in the most blasphemous terms. Finally there was Felicie Four—a dreamy, almost half-witted creature, distinctly pious and professedly clairvoyant, but this fourth personality was very unsatisfactory and elusive, and has been sometimes thought to be a deliberate trickery on the part of Felicie Three—a kind of joke played by her on a credulous public. I may say that, with the possible exception of Felicie Four each personality was distinct and separate and had no knowledge of the others. Felicie Two was undoubtedly the most predominant and would last sometimes for a fortnight at a time, then Felicie One would appear abruptly for a day or two. After that, perhaps, Felicie Three or Four, but the two latter seldom remained in command for more than a few hours. Each change was accompanied by severe headache and heavy sleep, and in each case there was complete loss of memory of the other states, the personality in question taking up life where she had left it, unconscious of the passage of time."

"Remarkable," murmured the Canon. "Very remarkable. As yet we know next to nothing of the marvels of the universe."

"We know that there are some very astute impostors in it," remarked the lawyer dryly.

"The case of Felicie Bault was investigated by lawyers as well as by doctors and scientists," said Dr. Campbell Clark quickly. "Maître Quimbellier, you remember, made the most thorough investigation and confirmed the views of the scientists. And after all, why should it surprise us so much? We come across the double-yolked egg, do we not?

And the twin banana? Why not the double soul—or in this case the quadruple soul—in the single body?"

"The double soul?" protested the Canon.

Dr. Campbell Clark turned his piercing blue eyes on him.

"What else can we call it? That is to say—if the personality is the soul?"

"It is a good thing such a state of affairs is only in the nature of a freak," remarked Sir George. "If the case were common, it would give rise to pretty complications."

"The condition is, of course, quite abnormal," agreed the doctor. "It was a great pity that a longer study could not have been made, but all that was put an end to by Felicie's unexpected death."

"There was something queer about that, if I remember rightly," said the lawyer slowly.

Dr. Campbell Clark nodded.

"A most unaccountable business. The girl was found one morning dead in bed. She had clearly been strangled. But to everyone's stupefaction it was presently proved beyond doubt that she had actually strangled herself. The marks on her neck were those of her own fingers. A method of suicide which, though not physically impossible, must have necessitated terrific muscular strength and almost superhuman will power. What had driven the girl to such straits has never been found out. Of course her mental balance must always have been precarious. Still, there it is. The curtain has been rung down forever on the mystery of Felicie Bault."

It was then that the man in the far corner laughed.

The other three men jumped as though shot. They had totally forgotten the existence of the fourth among them. As they stared toward the place where he sat, still hunched in his overcoat, he laughed again.

"You must excuse me, gentlemen," he said, in perfect English that had, nevertheless, a foreign flavor.

He sat up, displaying a pale face with a small jet-black mustache.

"Yes, you must excuse me," he said, with a mock bow. "But really! In science, is the last word ever said?"

"You know something of the case we have been discussing?" asked the doctor courteously.

"Of the case? No. But I knew her."

"Felicie Bault?"

"Yes. And Annette Ravel, also. You have not heard of Annette Ravel, I see? And yet the story of the one is the story of the other. Believe me, you know nothing of Felicie Bault if you do not also know the history of Annette Ravel."

He drew out a watch and looked at it.

"Just half an hour before the next stop. I have time to tell you the story—that is, if you care to hear it?"

"Please tell it to us," said the doctor quietly.

"Delighted," said the Canon. "Delighted."

Sir George Durand merely composed himself in an attitude of keen attention.

"My name, gentlemen," began their strange traveling companion, "is Raoul Letardeau. You have spoken just now of an English lady, Miss Slater, who interested herself in works of charity. I was born in that Brittany fishing village and when my parents were both killed in a railway accident it was Miss Slater who came to the rescue and saved me from the equivalent of your English workhouse. There were some twenty children under her care, girls and boys. Among these children were Felicie Bault and Annette Ravel. If I cannot make you understand the personality of Annette, gentlemen, you will understand nothing. She was the child of what you call a *fille de joie* who had died of consumption abandoned by her lover. The mother had been a dancer, and Annette, too, had the desire to dance. When I saw her first she was eleven years old, a little shrimp of a thing with eyes that alternately mocked and promised—a little creature all fire and life. And at once—yes, at once—she made me her slave. It was 'Raoul, do this for me.' 'Raoul, do that for me.' And me, I obeyed. Already I worshiped her, and she knew it.

"We would go down to the shore together, we three—for Felicie would come with us. And there Annette would pull off her shoes and stockings and dance on the sand. And then when she sank down breathless, she would tell us of what she meant to do and be.

" 'See you, I shall be famous. Yes, exceedingly famous. I will have hundreds and thousands of silk stockings—the finest silk. And I shall live in an exquisite apartment. All my lovers shall be young and handsome as well as being rich. And when I dance all Paris shall come to see me. They will yell and call and shout and go mad over my dancing. And in the winters I shall not dance. I shall go south to the sunlight. There are villas there with orange trees. I shall have one of them. I shall lie in the sun on silk cushions, eating oranges. As for you, Raoul, I will never forget you, however great and rich and famous I shall be. I will protect you and advance your career. Felicie here shall be my maid—no, her hands are too clumsy. Look at them, how large and coarse they are.'

"Felicie would grow angry at that. And then Annette would go on teasing her.

" 'She is so ladylike, Felicie—so elegant, so refined. She is a princess in disguise—ha, ha.'

" 'My father and mother were married, which is more than yours were,' Felicie would growl out spitefully.

" 'Yes, and your father killed your mother. A pretty thing, to be a murderer's daughter.'

" 'Your father left your mother to rot,' Felicie would rejoin.

" 'Ah, yes.' Annette became thoughtful. *'Pauvre Maman.* One must keep strong and well. It is everything to keep strong and well.'

" 'I am as strong as a horse,' Felicie boasted.

"And indeed she was. She had twice the strength of any other girl in the Home. And she was never ill.

"But she was stupid, you comprehend, stupid like a brute beast. I often wondered why she followed Annette round as she did. It was, with her, a kind of fascination. Sometimes, I think, she actually hated Annette, and indeed Annette was not kind to her. She jeered at her slowness and stupidity, and baited her in front of the others. I have seen Felicie grow quite white with rage. Sometimes I have thought that she would fasten her fingers round Annette's neck and choke the life out of her. She was not nimble-witted enough to reply to Annette's taunts, but she did learn in time to make one retort which never failed. That was the reference to her own health and strength. She had learned what I had always known, that Annette envied her her strong physique, and she struck instinctively at the weak spot in her enemy's armor.

"One day Annette came to me in great glee. 'Raoul,' she said, 'we shall have fun today with that stupid Felicie.'

" 'What are you going to do?'

" 'Come behind the little shed and I will tell you.'

"It seemed that Annette had got hold of some book. Part of it she did not understand, and indeed the whole thing was much over her head. It was an early work on hypnotism.

" 'A bright object, they say. The brass knob of my bed, it twirls round. I made Felicie look at it last night. "Look at it steadily," I said. "Do not take your eyes off it." And then I twirled it. Raoul, I was frightened. Her eyes looked so queer—so queer. "Felicie, you will do what I say always," I said. "I will do what you say always, Annette," she answered. And then—and then—I said, "Tomorrow you will bring a tallow candle out into the playground at twelve o'clock and start to eat it. And if anyone asks you, you will say that it is the best *galette* you ever tasted." Oh!

Raoul, think of it!'

" 'But she'll never do such a thing,' I objected.

" 'The book says so. Not that I can quite believe it—but, oh! Raoul, if the book is all true, how we shall amuse ourselves!'

"I, too, thought the idea very funny. We passed word round to the comrades and at twelve o'clock we were all in the playground. Punctual to the minute, out came Felicie with a stump of candle in her hand. Will you believe me, messieurs, she began solemnly to nibble at it. We were all in hysterics! Every now and then one or another of the children would go up to her and say solemnly, 'It is good, what you eat there, eh, Felicie?' And she would answer, 'But, yes, it is the best *galette* I ever tasted.' And then we would shriek with laughter. We laughed at last so loud that the noise seemed to wake up Felicie to a realization of what she was doing. She blinked her eyes in a puzzled way, looked at the candle, then at us. She passed her hand over her forehead.

" 'But what is it that I do here?' she muttered.

" 'You are eating a candle,' we screamed.

" '*I* made you do it. *I* made you do it,' cried Annette, dancing about.

"Felicie stared for a moment. Then she went slowly up to Annette.

" 'So it is you—it is you who have made me ridiculous? I seem to remember. Ah! I will kill you for this.'

"She spoke in a very quiet tone, but Annette rushed suddenly away and hid behind me.

" 'Save me, Raoul! I am afraid of Felicie. It was only a joke, Felicie. Only a joke.'

" 'I do not like these jokes,' said Felicie. 'You understand? I hate you. I hate you all.'

"She suddenly burst out crying and rushed away.

"Annette was, I think, scared by the result of her experiment, and did not try to repeat it. But from that day on her ascendency over Felicie seemed to grow stronger.

"Felicie, I now believe, always hated her, but nevertheless she could not keep away from her. She used to follow Annette around like a dog.

"Soon after that, messieurs, employment was found for me, and I only came to the home for occasional holidays. Annette's desire to become a dancer was not taken seriously, but she developed a very pretty singing voice as she grew older, and Miss Slater consented to her being trained as a singer.

"She was not lazy, Annette. She worked feverishly, without rest. Miss Slater was obliged to prevent her doing too much. She spoke to me once about her.

" 'You have always been fond of Annette,' she said. 'Persuade her not to work too hard. She has a little cough lately that I do not like.'

"My work took me far afield soon afterward. I received one or two letters from Annette at first, but then came silence. For five years after that I was abroad.

"Quite by chance, when I returned to Paris, my attention was caught by a poster advertising Annette Ravelli with a picture of the lady. I recognized her at once. That night I went to the theater in question. Annette sang in French and Italian. On the stage she was wonderful. Afterward I went to her dressing-room. She received me at once.

" 'Why, Raoul,' she cried, stretching out her whitened hands to me. 'This is splendid! Where have you been all these years?'

"I would have told her, but she did not really want to listen.

" 'You see, I have very nearly arrived!'

"She waved a triumphant hand round the room filled with bouquets.

" 'The good Miss Slater must be proud of your success.'

" 'That old one? No, indeed. She designed me, you know, for the Conservatoire. Decorous concert singing.

But me, I am an artist. It is here, on the variety stage, that I can express myself.'

"Just then a handsome middle-aged man came in. He was very distinguished. By his manner I soon saw that he was Annette's protector. He looked sideways at me, and Annette explained.

" 'A friend of my infancy. He passes through Paris, sees my picture on a poster, *et voilà!*'

"The man was then very affable and courteous. In my presence he produced a ruby-and-diamond bracelet and clasped it on Annette's wrist. As I rose to go, she threw me a glance of triumph and a whisper.

" 'I arrive, do I not? You see? All the world is before me.'

"But as I left the room, I heard her cough, a sharp, dry cough. I knew what it meant, that cough. It was the legacy of her consumptive mother.

"I saw her next two years later. She had gone for refuge to Miss Slater. Her career had broken down. She was in a state of advanced consumption for which the doctors said nothing could be done.

"Ah! I shall never forget her as I saw her then! She was lying in a kind of shelter in the garden. She was kept out-doors night and day. Her cheeks were hollow and flushed, her eyes bright and feverish.

"She greeted me with a kind of desperation that startled me.

" 'It is good to see you, Raoul. You know what they say— that I may not get well? They say it behind my back, you understand. To me they are soothing and consolatory. But it is not true, Raoul, it is not true! I shall not permit myself to die. Die? With beautiful life stretching in front of me? It is the will to live that matters. All the great doctors say that nowadays. I am not one of the feeble ones who let go. Already I feel myself infinitely better—infinitely better, do you hear?'

"She raised herself on her elbow to drive her words home, then fell back, attacked by a fit of coughing that racked her thin body.

"'The cough—it is nothing,' she gasped. 'And hemorrhages do not frighten me. I shall surprise the doctors. It is the will that counts. Remember, Raoul, I am going to live.'

"It was pitiful, you understand, pitiful.

"Just then, Felicie Bault came out with a tray. A glass of hot milk. She gave it to Annette and watched her drink it with an expression that I could not fathom. There was a kind of smug satisfaction in it.

"Annette, too, caught the look. She flung the glass down angrily, so that it smashed to bits.

"'You see her? That is how she always looks at me. She is glad I am going to die! Yes, she gloats over it. She who is well and strong. Look at her—never a day's illness, that one! And all for nothing. What good is that great carcass of hers to her? What can she make of it?'

"Felicie stooped and picked up the broken fragments of glass.

"'I do not mind what she says,' she observed in a singsong voice. 'What does it matter? I am a respectable girl, I am. As for her. She will be knowing the fires of Purgatory before very long. I am a Christian. I say nothing.'

"'You hate me!' cried Annette. 'You have always hated me. Ah! but I can charm you, all the same. I can make you do what I want. See now, if I asked you to, you would go down on your knees before me now on the grass.'

"'You are absurd,' said Felicie uneasily.

"'But, yes, you will do it. You will. To please me. Down on your knees. I ask it of you, I, Annette. Down on your knees, Felicie.'

"Whether it was the wonderful pleading in the voice, or some deeper motive, Felicie obeyed. She sank slowly on to her knees, her arms spread wide, her face vacant and stupid.

"Annette flung back her head and laughed—peal upon peal of laughter.

" 'Look at her, with her stupid face! How ridiculous she looks. You can get up now, Felicie, thank you! It is of no use to scowl at me. I am your mistress. You have to do what I say.'

"She lay back on her pillows exhausted. Felicie picked up the tray and moved slowly away. Once she looked back over her shoulder, and the smoldering resentment in her eyes startled me.

"I was not there when Annette died. But it was terrible, it seems. She clung to life. She fought against death like a madwoman. Again and again she gasped out, 'I will not die—do you hear me? I will not die. I will live—live—'

"Miss Slater told me all this when I came to see her six months later. 'My poor Raoul,' she said kindly. 'You loved her, did you not?'

" 'Always—always. But of what use could I be to her? Let us not talk of it. She is dead—she so brilliant, so full of burning life.'

"Miss Slater was a sympathetic woman. She went on to talk of other things. She was very worried about Felicie, so she told me. The girl had had a queer sort of nervous breakdown and ever since she had been very strange in manner.

" 'You know,' said Miss Slater, after a momentary hesitation, 'that she is learning the piano?'

"I did not know it and was very much surprised to hear it. Felicie—learning the piano! I would have declared the girl would not know one note from another.

" 'She has talent, they say,' continued Miss Slater. 'I can't understand it. I have always put her down as—well, Raoul, you know yourself, she was always a stupid girl.'

"I nodded.

" 'She is so strange in her manner I don't know what to make of it.'

"A few minutes later I entered the *salle de lecture*. Felicie was playing the piano. She was playing the air that I had heard Annette sing in Paris. You understand, messieurs, it gave me quite a turn. And then, hearing me, she broke off suddenly and looked round at me, her eyes full of mockery and intelligence. For a moment I thought— Well, I will not tell you what I thought.

" '*Tiens!*' she said. 'So it is you—Monsieur Raoul.'

"I cannot describe the way she said it. To Annette I had never ceased to be Raoul. But Felicie, since we had met as grown-ups, always addressed me as Monsieur Raoul. But the way she said it now was different—as though the *monsieur,* slightly stressed, was somehow amusing.

" 'Why, Felicie,' I stammered, 'you look quite different today.'

" 'Do I?' she said reflectively. 'It is odd, that. But do not be so solemn, Raoul—decidedly I shall call you Raoul—did we not play together as children?—Life was made for laughter. Let us talk of the poor Annette—she who is dead and buried. Is she in Purgatory, I wonder, or where?'

"And she hummed a snatch of song—untunefully enough, but the words caught my attention.

" 'Felicie!' I cried. 'You speak Italian?'

" 'Why not, Raoul? I am not as stupid as I pretend to be, perhaps.' She laughed at my mystification.

" 'I don't understand—' I began.

" 'But I will tell you. I am a very fine actress, though no one suspects it. I can play many parts—and play them very well.'

"She laughed again and ran quickly out of the room before I could stop her.

"I saw her again before I left. She was asleep in an armchair. She was snoring heavily. I stood and watched her, fascinated, yet repelled. Suddenly she woke with a start. Her eyes, dull and lifeless, met mine.

" 'Monsieur Raoul,' she muttered mechanically.

" 'Yes, Felicie. I am going now. Will you play for me again before I go?'

" 'I? Play? You are laughing at me, Monsieur Raoul.'

" 'Don't you remember playing for me this morning?'

"She shook her head.

" 'I play? How can a poor girl like me play?'

"She paused for a minute as though in thought, then beckoned me nearer.

" 'Monsieur Raoul, there are things going on in this house! They play tricks upon you. They alter the clocks. Yes, yes, I know what I am saying. And it is all her doing.'

" 'Whose doing?' I asked, startled.

" 'That Annette's. That wicked one's. When she was alive she always tormented me. Now that she is dead, she comes back from the dead to torment me.'

"I stared at Felicie. I could see now that she was in an extremity of terror, her eyes starting from her head.

" 'She is bad, that one. She is bad, I tell you. She would take the bread from your mouth, the clothes from your back, the soul from your body—'

"She clutched me suddenly.

" 'I am afraid, I tell you—afraid. I hear her voice—not in my ear—no, not in my ear. Here, in my head—' She tapped her forehead. 'She will drive me away—drive me away altogether, and then what shall I do, what will become of me?'

"Her voice rose almost to a shriek. She had in her eyes the look of the terrified beast at bay.

"Suddenly she smiled, a pleasant smile, full of cunning, with something in it that made me shiver.

" 'If it should come to it, Monsieur Raoul, I am very strong with my hands—very strong with my hands.'

"I had never noticed her hands particularly before. I looked at them now and shuddered in spite of myself. Squat, brutal fingers, and as Felicie had said, terribly strong. I cannot explain to you the nausea that swept over me. With hands such as these her father must have strangled her mother.

"That was the last time I ever saw Felicie Bault. Immediately afterward I went abroad—to South America. I returned from there two years after her death. Something I had read in the newspapers of her life and sudden death. I have heard fuller details tonight—from you. Felicie Three and Felicie Four—I wonder? She was a good actress, you know!"

The train suddenly slackened speed. The man in the corner sat erect and buttoned his overcoat more closely.

"What is your theory?" asked the lawyer, leaning forward.

"I can hardly believe—" began Canon Parfitt, and stopped.

The doctor said nothing. He was gazing steadily at Raoul Letardeau.

"The clothes from your back, the soul from your body," quoted the Frenchman lightly. He stood up. "I say to you, messieurs, that the history of Felicie Bault is the history of Annette Ravel. You did not know her, gentlemen. I did. She was very fond of life."

His hand on the door, ready to spring out, he turned suddenly and bending down tapped Canon Parfitt on the chest.

"*M. le docteur* over there, he said just now that all this" —his hand smote the Canon's stomach, and the Canon winced—"was only a residence. Tell me, if you find a burglar in your house what do you do? Shoot him, do you not?"

"No," cried the Canon. "No, indeed—I mean—not in this country."

But he spoke the last words to empty air. The carriage door banged.

The clergyman, the lawyer, and the doctor were alone. The fourth corner was vacant.

S.O.S.

"Ah!" said Mr. Dinsmead appreciatively. He stepped back and surveyed the round table with approval. The firelight gleamed on the coarse white tablecloth, the knives and forks, and the other table appointments.

"Is—is everything ready?" asked Mrs. Dinsmead hesitatingly. She was a little faded woman, with a colorless face, meager hair scraped back from her forehead, and a perpetually nervous manner.

"Everything's ready," said her husband with a kind of ferocious geniality.

He was a big man, with stooping shoulders and a broad red face. He had little pig's eyes that twinkled under his bushy brows, and a big jowl devoid of hair.

"Lemonade?" suggested Mrs. Dinsmead, almost in a whisper.

Her husband shook his head.

"Tea. Much better in every way. Look at the weather, streaming and blowing. A nice cup of hot tea is what's needed for supper on an evening like this."

He winked facetiously, then fell to surveying the table again.

"A good dish of eggs, cold corned beef, and bread and cheese. That's my order for supper. So come along and get it ready, Mother. Charlotte's in the kitchen waiting to give you a hand."

Mrs. Dinsmead rose, carefully winding up the ball of her knitting.

"She's grown a very good-looking girl," she murmured.

"Ah!" said Mr. Dinsmead. "The mortal image of her ma! So go along with you, and don't let's waste any more time."

He strolled about the room humming to himself for a minute or two. Once he approached the window and looked out.

"Wild weather," he murmured to himself. "Not much likelihood of our having visitors tonight."

Then he, too, left the room.

About ten minutes later Mrs. Dinsmead entered bearing a dish of fried eggs. Her two daughters followed, bringing the rest of the provisions. Mr. Dinsmead and his son Johnnie brought up the rear. The former seated himself at the head of the table.

"And for what we are to receive, et cetera," he remarked humorously. "And blessings on the man who first thought of tinned foods. What would we do, I should like to know, miles from anywhere, if we hadn't a tin now and then to fall back upon when the butcher forgets his weekly call?"

He proceeded to carve corned beef dexterously.

"I wonder who ever thought of building a house like this, miles from anywhere," said his daughter Magdalen, pettishly. "We never see a soul."

"No," said her father. "Never a soul."

"I can't think what made you take it, Father," said Charlotte.

"Can't you, my girl? Well, I had my reasons—I had my reasons."

His eyes sought his wife's furtively, but she frowned.

"And haunted, too," said Charlotte. "I wouldn't sleep alone here for anything."

"Pack of nonsense," said her father. "Never seen anything, have you?"

"Not seen anything perhaps, but—"

"But what?"

Charlotte did not reply, but she shivered a little. A great surge of rain came driving against the windowpane, and Mrs. Dinsmead dropped a spoon with a tinkle on the tray.

"Not nervous, are you, Mother?" said Mr. Dinsmead.

"It's a wild night, that's all. Don't you worry, we're safe here by our fireside, and not a soul from outside likely to disturb us. Why, it would be a miracle if anyone did. And miracles don't happen. No," he added as though to himself, with a kind of peculiar satisfaction, "miracles don't happen."

As the words left his lips there came a sudden knocking at the door. Mr. Dinsmead stayed as though petrified.

"What's that?" he muttered. His jaw fell.

Mrs. Dinsmead gave a little whimpering cry and pulled her shawl up round her. The color came into Magdalen's face and she leaned forward and spoke to her father.

"The miracle has happened," she said. "You'd better go and let whoever it is in."

Twenty minutes earlier Mortimer Cleveland had stood in the driving rain and mist surveying his car. It was really cursed bad luck. Two punctures within ten minutes of each other, and here he was, stranded, miles from anywhere, in the midst of these bare Wiltshire downs with night coming on and no prospect of shelter. Serve him right for trying to take a short cut. If only he had stuck to the main road! Now he was lost on what seemed a mere cart-track on the hillside, with no possibility of getting the car farther, and with no idea if there were even a village anywhere near.

He looked round him perplexedly, and his eye was caught by a gleam of light on the hillside above him. A second later the mist obscured it once more but, waiting patiently, he presently got a second glimpse of it. After a moment's cogitation, he left the car and struck up the side of the hill.

Soon he was out of the mist, and he recognized the light as shining from the lighted window of a small cottage. Here, at any rate, was shelter. Mortimer Cleveland quickened his pace, bending his head to meet the furious onslaught of wind and rain trying its best to drive him back.

Cleveland was, in his own way, something of a celebrity though doubtless the majority of folks would have displayed complete ignorance of his name and achievements. He was an authority on mental science and had written two excellent textbooks on the subconscious. He was also a member of the Psychical Research Society and a student of the occult in so far as it affected his own conclusions and line of research.

He was by nature peculiarly susceptible to atmosphere, and by deliberate training he had increased his own natural gift. When he had at last reached the cottage and rapped at the door, he was conscious of an excitement, a quickening of interest, as though all his faculties had suddenly been sharpened.

The murmur of voices within had been plainly audible to him. Upon his knock there came a sudden silence, then the sound of a chair being pushed back along the floor. In another minute the door was flung open by a boy of about fifteen. Cleveland could look straight over his shoulder upon the scene within.

It reminded him of an interior by some Dutch painter. A round table spread for a meal, a family party sitting round it, one or two flickering candles and the firelight's glow over all. The father, a big man, sat at one side of the table, a little gray woman with a frightened face sat opposite him. Facing the door, looking straight at Cleveland, was a girl. Her startled eyes looked straight into his, her hand with a cup in it was arrested halfway to her lips.

She was, Cleveland saw at once, a beautiful girl of an extremely uncommon type. Her hair, red gold, stood out round her face like a mist; her eyes, very far apart, were a pure gray. She had the mouth and chin of an early Italian Madonna.

There was a moment's dead silence. Then Cleveland stepped into the room and explained his predicament. He brought his trite story to a close, and there was another pause harder to understand. At last, as though with an effort, the father rose.

"Come in, sir—Mr. Cleveland, did you say?"

"That is my name," said Mortimer, smiling.

"Ah, yes. Come in, Mr. Cleveland. Not weather for a dog outside, is it? Come in by the fire. Shut the door, can't you, Johnnie? Don't stand there half the night."

Cleveland came forward and sat on a wooden stool by the fire. The boy Johnnie shut the door.

"Dinsmead, that's my name," said the other man. He was all geniality now. "This is the Missus, and these are my two daughters, Charlotte and Magdalen."

For the first time, Cleveland saw the face of the girl who had been sitting with her back to him, and saw that, in a totally different way, she was quite as beautiful as her sister. Very dark, with a face of marble pallor, a delicate aquiline nose, and a grave mouth. It was a kind of frozen beauty, austere and almost forbidding. She acknowledged her father's introduction by bending her head, and she looked at him with an intent gaze that was searching in character. It was as though she were summing him up, weighing him in the balance of her clear young judgment.

"A drop of something to drink, eh, Mr. Cleveland?"

"Thank you," said Mortimer. "A cup of tea will meet the case admirably."

Mr. Dinsmead hesitated a minute, then he picked up the five cups, one after another, from the table and emptied them into the slop bowl.

"This tea's cold," he said brusquely. "Make us some more, will you, Mother?"

Mrs. Dinsmead got up quickly and hurried off with the teapot. Mortimer had an idea that she was glad to get out of the room.

The fresh tea soon came, and the unexpected guest was plied with viands.

Mr. Dinsmead talked and talked. He was expansive, genial, loquacious. He told the stranger all about himself. He'd lately retired from the building trade—yes, made quite a good thing out of it. He and the Missus thought they'd like a bit of country air—never lived in the country before. Wrong time of year to choose, of course, October and November, but they didn't want to wait. "Life's uncertain, you know, sir." So they had taken this cottage. Eight miles from anywhere, and nineteen miles from anything you could call a town. No, they didn't complain. The girls found it a bit dull, but he and Mother enjoyed the quiet.

So he talked on, leaving Mortimer almost hypnotized by the easy flow. Nothing here, surely, but rather commonplace domesticity. And yet, at that first glimpse of the interior, he had diagnosed something else, some tension, some strain, emanating from one of those four people—he didn't know which. Mere foolishness, his nerves were all awry! They were startled by his sudden appearance—that was all.

He broached the question of a night's lodging, and was met with a ready response.

"You'll have to stop with us, Mr. Cleveland. Nothing else for miles round. We can give you a bedroom, and though my pajamas may be a bit roomy, why, they're better than nothing, and your own clothes will be dry by morning."

"It's very good of you."

"Not at all," said the other genially. "As I said just now, one couldn't turn away a dog on a night like this. Magdalen, Charlotte, go up and see to the room."

The two girls left the room. Presently Mortimer heard them moving about overhead.

"I can quite understand that two attractive young ladies like your daughters might find it dull here," said Cleveland.

"Good lookers, aren't they?" said Mr. Dinsmead with fatherly pride. "Not much like their mother or myself. We're a homely pair, but much attached to each other, I'll tell you that, Mr. Cleveland. Eh, Maggie, isn't that so?"

Mrs. Dinsmead smiled primly. She had started knitting again. The needles clicked busily. She was a fast knitter.

Presently the room was announced ready, and Mortimer, expressing thanks once more, declared his intention of turning in.

"Did you put a hot-water bottle in the bed?" demanded Mrs. Dinsmead, suddenly mindful of her house pride.

"Yes, Mother, two."

"That's right," said Dinsmead. "Go up with him, girls, and see that everything is all right."

Magdalen preceded him up the staircase, her candle held aloft. Charlotte came behind.

The room was quite a pleasant one, small and with a sloping roof, but the bed looked comfortable, and the few pieces of somewhat dusty furniture were of old mahogany. A large can of hot water stood in the basin, a pair of pink pajamas of ample proportions were laid over a chair, and the bed was made and turned down.

Magdalen went over to the window and saw that the fastenings were secure. Charlotte cast a final eye over the washstand appointments. Then they both lingered by the door.

"Good night, Mr. Cleveland. You are sure there is everything?"

"Yes, thank you, Miss Magdalen. I am sorry to have given you both so much trouble. Good night."

"Good night."

They went out, shutting the door behind them. Mortimer Cleveland was alone. He undressed slowly and thoughtfully. When he had donned Mr. Dinsmead's pink pajamas, he gathered up his own wet clothes and put them outside the door as his host had bade him. From downstairs he could hear the rumble of Dinsmead's voice.

What a talker the man was! Altogether an odd personality—but indeed there was something odd about the whole family, or was it his imagination?

He went slowly back into his room and shut the door. He stood by the bed lost in thought. And then he started—

The mahogany table by the bed was smothered in dust. Written in the dust were three letters clearly visible. *S.O.S.*

Mortimer stared as if he could hardly believe his eyes. It was a confirmation of all his vague surmises and forebodings. He was right, then. Something was wrong in this house.

S.O.S. A call for help. But whose finger had written it in the dust? Magdalen's or Charlotte's? They had both stood there, he remembered, for a moment or two, before going out of the room. Whose hand had secretly dropped to the table and traced out those three letters?

The faces of the two girls came up before him. Magdalen's, dark and aloof, and Charlotte's, as he had seen it first, wide-eyed, startled, with an unfathomable something in her glance.

He went again to the door and opened it. The boom of Mr. Dinsmead's voice was no longer to be heard. The house was silent.

He thought to himself, *I can do nothing tonight. Tomorrow—well, we shall see.*

Cleveland woke early. He went down through the living-room, and out into the garden. The morning was fresh and beautiful after the rain. Someone else was up early, too. At the bottom of the garden Charlotte was leaning on the fence staring out over the Downs. His pulses quickened a little as he went down to join her. All along he had been secretly convinced that it was Charlotte who had written the message. As he came up to her, she turned and wished him good morning. Her eyes were direct and childlike, with no hint of a secret understanding in them.

"A very good morning," said Mortimer, smiling. "The weather this morning is a contrast to last night's."

"It is indeed."

Mortimer broke off a twig from a tree near by. With it he began idly to draw on the smooth, sandy patch at his feet. He traced an S, then an O, then an S, watching the girl narrowly as he did so. But again he could detect no gleam of comprehension.

"Do you know what these letters represent?" he said abruptly.

Charlotte frowned a little. "Aren't they what boats send out when they are in distress?" she asked.

Mortimer nodded. "Someone wrote that on the table by my bed last night," he said quietly. "I thought perhaps you might have done so."

She looked at him in wide-eyed astonishment.

"I? Oh, no."

He was wrong, then. A sharp pang of disappointment shot through him. He had been so sure—so sure. It was not often that his intuitions led him astray.

"You are quite certain?" he persisted.

"Oh, yes."

They turned and went slowly together toward the house. Charlotte seemed preoccupied about something. She replied at random to the few observations he made. Suddenly she burst out in a low, hurried voice, "It—it's odd your asking that about those letters, S.O.S. I didn't write them, of course, but—I so easily might have."

He stopped and looked at her, and she went on quickly. "It sounds silly, I know, but I have been so frightened, so dreadfully frightened, and when you came in last night, it seemed like an—an answer to something."

"What are you frightened of?" he asked quickly.

"I don't know."

"You don't know?"

"I think—it's the house. Ever since we came here it has been growing and growing. Everyone seems different somehow. Father, Mother, and Magdalen, they all seem different."

Mortimer did not speak at once, and before he could do so, Charlotte went on again.

"You know this house is supposed to be haunted?"

"What?" All his interest was quickened.

"Yes, a man murdered his wife in it, oh, some years ago now. We only found out about it after we got here. Father says ghosts are all nonsense, but I—don't know."

Mortimer was thinking rapidly. "Tell me," he said in a businesslike tone, "was this murder committed in the room I had last night?"

"I don't know anything about that," said Charlotte.

"I wonder, now," said Mortimer half to himself, "yes, that may be it."

Charlotte looked at him uncomprehendingly.

"Miss Dinsmead," said Mortimer gently, "have you ever had any reason to believe that you are mediumistic?"

She stared at him.

"I think you know that you did write S.O.S. last night," he said quietly. "Oh, quite unconsciously, of course. A crime stains the atmosphere, so to speak. A sensitive mind such as yours might be acted upon in such a manner. You have been reproducing the sensations and impressions of the victim. Many years ago *she* may have written S.O.S. on that table, and you unconsciously reproduced her act last night."

Charlotte's face brightened. "I see," she said. "You think that is the explanation?"

A voice called her from the house, and she went in, leaving Mortimer to pace up and down the garden paths. Was he satisfied with his own explanation? Did it cover the facts as he knew them? Did it account for the tension he had felt on entering the house last night?

Perhaps, and yet he still had the odd feeling that his sudden appearance had produced something very like consternation. He thought to himself, *I must not be carried away by the psychic explanation. It might account for Charlotte—but not for the others. My coming as I did upset them horribly, all except Johnnie. Whatever it is that's the matter, Johnnie is out of it.*

He was quite sure of that; strange that he should be so positive, but there it was.

At that minute Johnnie himself came out of the cottage and approached the guest.

"Breakfast's ready," he said awkwardly. "Will you come in?"

Mortimer noticed that the lad's fingers were much stained. Johnnie felt his glance and laughed ruefully.

"I'm always messing about with chemicals, you know," he said. "It makes Dad awfully wild sometimes. He wants me to go into building, but I want to do chemistry and research work."

Mr. Dinsmead appeared at the window ahead of them, broad, jovial, smiling, and at sight of him all Mortimer's distrust and antagonism reawakened. Mrs. Dinsmead was already seated at the table. She wished him good morning in her colorless voice, and he had again the impression that for some reason or other, she was afraid of him.

Magdalen came in last. She gave him a brief nod and took her seat opposite him.

"Did you sleep well?" she asked abruptly. "Was your bed comfortable?"

She looked at him very earnestly, and when he replied courteously in the affirmative he noticed something very like a flicker of disappointment pass over her face. What had she expected him to say, he wondered?

He turned to his host. "This lad of yours is interested in chemistry, it seems," he said pleasantly.

There was a crash. Mrs. Dinsmead had dropped her teacup.

"Now then, Maggie, now then," said her husband.

It seemed to Mortimer that there was admonition, warning, in his voice. He turned to his guest and spoke fluently of the advantages of the building trade, and of not letting young boys get above themselves.

After breakfast he went out in the garden by himself, and smoked. The time was clearly at hand when he must leave the cottage. A night's shelter was one thing; to prolong it was difficult without an excuse, and what possible excuse could he offer? And yet he was singularly loath to depart.

Turning the thing over and over in his mind, he took a path that led round the other side of the house. His shoes were soled with crepe rubber, and made little or no noise. He was passing the kitchen window when he heard Dinsmead's words from within, and the words attracted his attention immediately.

"It's a fair lump of money, it is."

Mrs. Dinsmead's voice answered. It was too faint in tone for Mortimer to hear the words, but Dinsmead replied, "Nigh on sixty thousand pounds, the lawyer said."

Mortimer had no intention of eavesdropping, but he retraced his steps very thoughtfully. The mention of money seemed to crystallize the situation. Somewhere or other there was a question of £60,000. It made the thing clearer —and uglier.

Magdalen came out of the house, but her father's voice called her almost immediately, and she went in again. Presently Dinsmead himself joined his guest.

"Rare good morning," he said genially. "I hope your car will be none the worse."

Wants to find out when I'm going, thought Mortimer to himself. Aloud he thanked Mr. Dinsmead once more for his timely hospitality.

"Not at all, not at all," said the other.

Magdalen and Charlotte came together out of the house and strolled arm in arm to a rustic seat some little distance away. The dark head and the golden one made a pleasant contrast together and on an impulse Mortimer said, "Your daughters are very unlike, Mr. Dinsmead."

The other who was just lighting his pipe gave a sharp jerk of the wrist and dropped the match.

"Do you think so?" he asked. "Yes, well, I suppose they are."

Mortimer had a flash of intuition. "But of course they are not both your daughters," he said smoothly.

He saw Dinsmead look at him, hesitate for a moment, and then make up his mind.

"That's very clever of you, sir," he said. "No, one of them is a foundling; we took her in as a baby and we have brought her up as our own. She herself has not the least idea of the truth, but she'll have to know soon." He sighed.

"A question of inheritance?" suggested Mortimer quietly.

The other flashed a suspicious look at him. Then he decided that frankness was best; his manner became almost aggressively frank and open.

"It's odd you should say that, sir."

"A case of telepathy, eh?" said Mortimer, and smiled.

"It is like this, sir. We took her in to oblige the mother—for a consideration, as at the time I was just starting in the building trade. A few months ago I noticed an advertisement in the papers, and it seemed to me that the child in question must be our Magdalen. I went to see the lawyers, and there has been a lot of talk one way and another. They were suspicious—naturally, as you might say—but everything is cleared up now. I am taking the girl herself to London next week—she doesn't know anything about it so far. Her father, it seems, was a very rich man. He only learned of the child's existence a few months before his death. He hired agents to try and trace her, and left all his money to her when she should be found."

Mortimer listened with close attention. He had no reason to doubt Mr. Dinsmead's story. It explained Magdalen's dark beauty; explained, too, perhaps, her aloof manner. Nevertheless, though the story itself might be true, something lay undivulged behind it.

But Mortimer had no intention of rousing the other's suspicions. Instead, he must go out of his way to allay them.

"A very interesting story, Mr. Dinsmead," he said. "I congratulate Miss Magdalen. An heiress and a beauty, she has a great future ahead."

"She has that," agreed her father warmly, "and she's a rare good girl, too, Mr. Cleveland."

There was every evidence of hearty warmth in his manner.

"Well," said Mortimer, "I must be pushing along now, I suppose. I have got to thank you once more, Mr. Dinsmead, for your singularly well-timed hospitality."

Accompanied by his host, he went into the house to bid farewell to Mrs. Dinsmead. She was standing by the window with her back to them, and did not hear them enter. At her husband's jovial, "Here's Mr. Cleveland come to say good-by," she started nervously and swung round, dropping something which she held in her hand. Mortimer picked it up for her. It was a miniature of Charlotte done in the style of some twenty-five years ago. Mortimer repeated to her the thanks he had already proffered to her husband. He noticed again her look of fear and the furtive glances that she shot at him beneath her eyelids.

The two girls were not in evidence, but it was not part of Mortimer's policy to seem anxious to see them; also he had his own idea, which was shortly to prove correct.

He had gone about half a mile from the house on his way down to where he had left the car the night before, when the bushes on one side of the path were thrust aside, and Magdalen came out on the track ahead of him.

"I had to see you," she said.

"I expected you," said Mortimer. "It was you who wrote S.O.S. on the table in my room last night, wasn't it?"

Magdalen nodded.

"Why?" asked Mortimer gently.

The girl turned aside and began pulling off leaves from a bush.

"I don't know," she said. "Honestly, I don't know."

"Tell me," said Mortimer.

Magdalen drew a deep breath.

"I am a practical person," she said, "not the kind of person who imagines things or fancies them. You, I think, believe in ghosts and spirits. I don't, and when I tell you that there is something very wrong in that house," she pointed up the hill, "I mean that there is something tangibly wrong—it's not just an echo of the past. It has been coming on ever since we've been there. Every day it grows worse. Father is different, Mother is different, Charlotte is different."

Mortimer interposed. "Is Johnnie different?" he asked.

Magdalen looked at him, a dawning appreciation in her eyes. "No," she said, "now I come to think of it, Johnnie is not different. He is the only one who's—who's untouched by it all. He was untouched last night at tea."

"And you?" asked Mortimer.

"I was afraid—horribly afraid, just like a child—without knowing what it was I was afraid of. And Father was—queer, there's no other word for it. He talked about miracles and then I prayed—actually prayed for a miracle, and *you* knocked on the door."

She stopped abruptly, staring at him. "I seem mad to you, I suppose," she said defiantly.

"No," said Mortimer, "on the contrary you seem extremely sane. All sane people have a premonition of danger if it is near them."

"You don't understand," said Magdalen. "I was not afraid—for myself."

"For whom, then?"

But again Magdalen shook her head in a puzzled fashion. "I don't know."

She went on. "I wrote S.O.S. on an impulse. I had an idea —absurd, no doubt—that they would not let me speak to you—the rest of them, I mean. I don't know what it was I meant to ask you to do. I don't know now."

"Never mind," said Mortimer. "I shall do it."

"What can you do?"

Mortimer smiled a little. "I can think."

She looked at him doubtfully.

"Yes," said Mortimer, "a lot can be done that way, more than you would ever believe. Tell me, was there any chance word or phrase that attracted your attention just before that meal last evening?"

Magdalen frowned. "I don't think so," she said.

"At least I heard Father saying something to Mother about Charlotte being the living image of her, and he laughed in a very queer way, but—there's nothing odd in that, is there?"

"No," said Mortimer slowly, "except that Charlotte is not like your mother."

He remained lost in thought for a minute or two, then looked up to find Magdalen watching him uncertainly.

"Go home, child," he said, "and don't worry. Leave it in my hands."

She went obediently up the path toward the cottage. Mortimer strolled on a little farther, then threw himself down on the green turf. He closed his eyes, detached himself from conscious thought or effort, and let a series of pictures flit at will across the surface of his mind.

Johnnie! He always came back to Johnnie. Johnnie, completely innocent, utterly free from all the network of suspicion and intrigue, but nevertheless the pivot around which everything turned. He remembered the crash of Mrs. Dinsmead's cup on her saucer at breakfast that morning. What had caused her agitation? A chance reference on his part to the lad's fondness for chemicals? At the moment he had not been conscious of Mr. Dinsmead, but he saw him now clearly, as he sat, his teacup poised halfway to his lips.

That took him back to Charlotte, as he had seen her when the door opened last night. She had sat staring at him over the rim of her teacup. And swiftly on that followed another memory. Mr. Dinsmead emptying teacups one after the other, and saying, "This tea's cold."

He remembered the steam that went up. Surely the tea had not been so very cold after all?

Something began to stir in his brain. A memory of something read not so very long ago, within a month perhaps. Some account of a whole family poisoned by a lad's carelessness. A packet of arsenic left in the larder had sifted through to the bread below. He had read it in the paper. Probably Mr. Dinsmead had read it, too.

Things began to grow clearer.

Half an hour later, Mortimer Cleveland rose briskly to his feet.

It was evening once more in the cottage. The eggs were poached tonight and there was a tin of brawn. Presently Mrs. Dinsmead came in from the kitchen bearing the big teapot. The family took their places round the table.

Mrs. Dinsmead filled the cups and handed them round the table. Then, as she put the teapot down, she gave a sudden little cry and pressed her hand to her heart. Mr. Dinsmead swung round in his chair, following the direction of her terrified eyes. Mortimer Cleveland was standing in the doorway.

He came forward. His manner was pleasant and apologetic.

"I'm afraid I startled you," he said. "I had to come back for something."

"Back for something," cried Mr. Dinsmead. His face was purple, his veins swelling. "Back for what, I should like to know?"

"Some tea," said Mortimer.

With a swift gesture he took something from his pocket and taking up one of the teacups from the table, emptied some of its contents into a little test tube he held in his left hand.

"What—what are you doing?" gasped Mr. Dinsmead. His face had gone chalky-white, the purple dying out as if by magic. Mrs. Dinsmead gave a thin, high, frightened cry.

"You read the papers, Mr. Dinsmead? I am sure you do. Sometimes one reads accounts of a whole family being poisoned—some of them recover, some do not. In this case, one would not. The first explanation would be the tinned brawn you were eating, but supposing the doctor to be a suspicious man, not easily taken in by the tinned food theory? There is a packet of arsenic in your larder. On the shelf below it is a packet of tea. There is a convenient hole in the top shelf. What more natural to suppose than that the arsenic found its way into the tea by accident? Your son Johnnie might be blamed for carelessness, nothing more."

"I—I don't know what you mean," gasped Dinsmead.

"I think you do." Mortimer took up a second teacup and filled a second test tube. He fixed a red label to one and a blue label to the other.

"The red-labeled one," he said, "contains tea from your daughter Charlotte's cup, the other from your daughter Magdalen's. I am prepared to swear that in the first I shall find four or five times the amount of arsenic than in the latter."

"You are mad!" said Dinsmead.

"Oh, dear me, no. I am nothing of the kind. You told me today, Mr. Dinsmead, that Magdalen was not your own daughter. You lied to me. Magdalen *is* your daughter. Charlotte was the child you adopted, the child who was so like her mother that when I held a miniature of that mother in my hand today I mistook it for one of Charlotte herself. You wanted your own daughter to inherit the fortune, and since it might be impossible to keep Charlotte out of sight, and someone who knew her mother might have realized the truth of the resemblance, you decided on, well—sufficient white arsenic at the bottom of a tea-cup."

Mrs. Dinsmead gave a sudden high cackle, rocking herself to and fro in violent hysterics.

"Tea," she squeaked, "that's what he said, tea, not lemonade."

"Hold your tongue, can't you?" roared her husband wrathfully.

Mortimer saw Charlotte looking at him, wide-eyed, wondering, across the table. Then he felt a hand on his arm, and Magdalen dragged him out of earshot.

"Those," she pointed at the phials—"Daddy. You won't—"

Mortimer laid his hand on her shoulder. "My child," he said, "you don't believe in the past. I do. I believe in the atmosphere of this house. If he had not come to this particular house, perhaps—I say *perhaps*—your father might not have conceived the plan he did. I will keep these two test tubes to safeguard Charlotte now and in the future. Apart from that, I shall do nothing—in gratitude, if you will, to the hand that wrote S.O.S."

WHERE THERE'S A WILL

"ABOVE ALL, AVOID WORRY AND EXCITEMENT," said Dr. Meynell, in the comfortable fashion affected by doctors.

Mrs. Harter, as is often the case with people hearing these soothing but meaningless words, seemed more doubtful than relieved.

"There is a certain cardiac weakness," continued the doctor fluently, "but nothing to be alarmed about. I can assure you of that. All the same," he added, "it might be as well to have an elevator installed. Eh? What about it?"

Mrs. Harter looked worried.

Dr. Meynell, on the contrary, looked pleased with himself. The reason he liked attending rich patients rather than poor ones was that he could exercise his active imagination in prescribing for their ailments.

"Yes, an elevator," said Dr. Meynell, trying to think of something else even more dashing—and failing. "Then we shall avoid all undue exertion. Daily exercise on the level on a fine day, but avoid walking up hills. And, above all, plenty of distraction for the mind. Don't dwell on your health."

To the old lady's nephew, Charles Ridgeway, the doctor was slightly more explicit.

"Do not misunderstand me," he said. "Your aunt may live for years, probably will. At the same time, shock or overexertion might carry her off like that!" He snapped his fingers. "She must lead a very quiet life. No exertion. No fatigue. But, of course, she must not be allowed to brood. She must be kept cheerful and the mind well distracted."

"Distracted," said Charles Ridgeway thoughtfully.

Charles was a thoughtful young man. He was also a

young man who believed in furthering his own inclinations whenever possible.

That evening he suggested the installation of a radio set.

Mrs. Harter, already seriously upset at the thought of the elevator, was disturbed and unwilling. Charles was persuasive.

"I do not know that I care for these new-fangled things," said Mrs. Harter piteously. "The waves, you know—the electric waves. They might affect me."

Charles, in a superior and kindly fashion, pointed out the futility of this idea.

Mrs. Harter, whose knowledge of the subject was of the vaguest but who was tenacious of her own opinion, remained unconvinced.

"All that electricity," she murmured timorously. "You may say what you like, Charles, but some people are affected by electricity. I always have a terrible headache before a thunderstorm. I know that." She nodded her head triumphantly.

Charles was a patient young man. He was also persistent.

"My dear Aunt Mary," he said, "let me make the thing clear to you."

He was something of an authority on the subject. He delivered quite a lecture on the theme; warming to his task, he spoke of bright-emitter tubes, of dull-emitter tubes, of high frequency and low frequency, of amplification and of condensers.

Mrs. Harter, submerged in a sea of words that she did not understand, surrendered.

"Of course, Charles," she murmured, "if you really think—"

"My dear Aunt Mary," said Charles enthusiastically, "it is the very thing for you, to keep you from moping and all that."

The elevator prescribed by Dr. Meynell was installed

shortly afterward and was very nearly the death of Mrs. Harter since, like many other old ladies, she had a rooted objection to strange men in the house. She suspected them one and all of having designs on her old silver.

After the elevator the radio set arrived. Mrs. Harter was left to contemplate the, to her, repellent object—a large, ungainly-looking box, studded with knobs.

It took all Charles's enthusiasm to reconcile her to it, but Charles was in his element, turning knobs and discoursing eloquently.

Mrs. Harter sat in her high-backed chair, patient and polite, with a rooted conviction in her own mind that these new-fangled notions were neither more nor less than unmitigated nuisances.

"Listen, Aunt Mary, we are on to Berlin! Isn't that splendid? Can you hear the fellow?"

"I can't hear anything except a good deal of buzzing and clicking," said Mrs. Harter.

Charles continued to twirl knobs. "Brussels," he announced with enthusiasm.

"Is it really?" said Mrs. Harter with no more than a trace of interest.

Charles again turned knobs and an unearthly howl echoed forth into the room.

"Now we seem to be on to the Dogs' Home," said Mrs. Harter, who was an old lady with a certain amount of spirit.

"Ha, ha!" said Charles, "you will have your joke, won't you, Aunt Mary? Very good that!"

Mrs. Harter could not help smiling at him. She was very fond of Charles. For some years a niece, Miriam Harter, had lived with her. She had intended to make the girl her heiress, but Miriam had not been a success. She was impatient and obviously bored by her aunt's society. She was always out, "gadding about" as Mrs. Harter called it. In the end she had entangled herself with a young man of whom her aunt thoroughly disapproved. Miriam had been returned to her mother with a curt note much as if she had been goods on approval. She had married the young man in question and Mrs. Harter usually sent her a handkerchief case or a table center at Christmas.

Having found nieces disappointing, Mrs. Harter turned her attention to nephews. Charles, from the first, had been an unqualified success. He was always pleasantly deferential to his aunt and listened with an appearance of intense interest to the reminiscences of her youth. In this he was a great contrast to Miriam who had been frankly bored and showed it. Charles was never bored; he was always goodtempered, always gay. He told his aunt many times a day that she was a perfectly marvelous old lady.

Highly satisfied with her new acquisition, Mrs. Harter had written to her lawyer with instructions as to the making of a new will. This was sent to her, duly approved by her, and signed.

And now even in the matter of the radio, Charles was soon proved to have won fresh laurels.

Mrs. Harter, at first antagonistic, became tolerant and finally fascinated. She enjoyed it very much better when Charles was out. The trouble with Charles was that he could not leave the thing alone. Mrs. Harter would be seated in her chair comfortably listening to a symphony concert or a lecture on Lucrezia Borgia or Pond Life, quite happy and at peace with the world. Not so Charles. The harmony would be shattered by discordant shrieks while he enthusiastically attempted to get foreign stations. But on those evenings when Charles was dining out with friends, Mrs. Harter enjoyed the radio very much indeed. She would turn on two switches, sit in her high-backed chair, and enjoy the program of the evening.

It was about three months after the radio had been installed that the first eerie happening occurred. Charles was absent at a bridge party.

The program for that evening was a ballad concert. A well-known soprano was singing *Annie Laurie,* and in the middle of *Annie Laurie* a strange thing happened. There was a sudden break, the music ceased for a moment, the buzzing, clicking noise continued, and then that, too, died away. There was silence, and then very faintly a low buzzing sound was heard.

Mrs. Harter got the impression, why she did not know, that the machine was tuned into somewhere very far away, and then, clearly and distinctly, a voice spoke, a man's voice with a faint Irish accent.

"Mary—can you hear me, Mary? It is Patrick speaking. . . . I am coming for you soon. You will be ready, won't you, Mary?"

Then, almost immediately, the strains of *Annie Laurie* once more filled the room.

Mrs. Harter sat rigid in her chair, her hands clenched on each arm of it. Had she been dreaming? Patrick! Patrick's voice! Patrick's voice in this very room, speaking to her. No, it must be a dream, a hallucination perhaps. She must just have dropped off to sleep for a minute or two. A curious thing to have dreamed—that her dead husband's voice should speak to her over the ether. It frightened her just a little. What were the words he had said?

"I am coming for you soon. You will be ready, won't you, Mary?"

Was it, could it be a premonition? Cardiac weakness. Her heart. After all, she was getting on in years.

"It's a warning—that's what it is," said Mrs. Harter, rising slowly and painfully from her chair, and added characteristically, "All that money wasted on putting in an elevator!"

She said nothing of her experience to anyone, but for the next day or two she was thoughtful and a little preoccupied.

And then came the second occasion. Again she was alone

in the room. The radio, which had been playing an orchestral selection, died away with the same suddenness as before. Again there was silence, the sense of distance, and finally Patrick's voice, not as it had been in life—but a voice rarefied, faraway, with a strange unearthly quality.

"Patrick speaking to you, Mary. I will be coming for you very soon now—"

Then click, buzz, and the orchestral selection was in full swing again.

Mrs. Harter glanced at the clock. No, she had not been asleep this time. Awake and in full possession of her faculties, she had heard Patrick's voice speaking. It was no hallucination, she was sure of that. In a confused way she tried to think over all that Charles had explained to her of the theory of ether waves.

Could it be that Patrick had really spoken to her? That his actual voice had been wafted through space? There were missing wave lengths or something of that kind. She remembered Charles speaking of "gaps in the scale." Perhaps the missing waves explained all the so-called psychological phenomena? No, there was nothing inherently impossible in the idea. Patrick had spoken to her. He had availed himself of modern science to prepare her for what must soon be coming.

Mrs. Harter rang the bell for her maid, Elizabeth.

Elizabeth was a tall, gaunt woman of sixty. Beneath an unbending exterior she concealed a wealth of affection and tenderness for her mistress.

"Elizabeth," said Mrs. Harter when her faithful retainer had appeared, "you remember what I told you? The top left-hand drawer of my bureau. It is locked—the long key with the white label. Everything there is ready."

"Ready, ma'am?"

"For my burial," snorted Mrs. Harter. "You know perfectly well what I mean, Elizabeth. You helped me to put the things there yourself."

Elizabeth's face began to work strangely. "Oh, ma'am," she wailed, "don't dwell on such things. I thought you was a sight better."

"We have all got to go sometime or another," said Mrs. Harter practically. "I am over my three score years and ten, Elizabeth. There, there, don't make a fool of yourself. If you must cry, go and cry somewhere else."

Elizabeth retired, still sniffing.

Mrs. Harter looked after her with a good deal of affection.

"Silly old fool, but faithful," she said, "very faithful. Let me see, was it a hundred pounds, or only fifty I left her? It ought to be a hundred."

The point worried the old lady and the next day she sat down and wrote to her lawyer asking if he would send her her will so that she might look it over. It was that same day that Charles startled her by something he said at lunch.

"By the way, Aunt Mary," he said, "who is that funny old josser up in the spare room? The picture over the mantelpiece, I mean. The old johnny with the beaver and side whiskers?"

Mrs. Harter looked at him austerely.

"That is your Uncle Patrick as a young man," she said.

"Oh, I say, Aunt Mary, I am awfully sorry. I didn't mean to be rude."

Mrs. Harter accepted the apology with a dignified bend of the head.

Charles went on rather uncertainly, "I just wondered. You see—"

He stopped undecidedly and Mrs. Harter said sharply, "Well? What were you going to say?"

"Nothing," said Charles hastily. "Nothing that makes sense, I mean."

For the moment the old lady said nothing more, but later that day, when they were alone together, she returned to the subject.

"I wish you would tell me, Charles, what it was that made you ask me about the picture of your uncle."

Charles looked embarrassed.

"I told you, Aunt Mary. It was nothing but a silly fancy of mine—quite absurd."

"Charles," said Mrs. Harter in her most autocratic voice, "I insist upon knowing."

"Well, my dear aunt, if you will have it, I fancied I saw him—the man in the picture, I mean—looking out of the end window when I was coming up the drive last night. Some effect of the light, I suppose. I wondered who on earth he could be, the face was so—early Victorian, if you know what I mean. And then Elizabeth said there was no one, no visitor or stranger in the house, and later in the evening I happened to drift into the spare room, and there was the picture over the mantelpiece. My man to the life! It is quite easily explained, really, I expect. Subconscious and all that. Must have noticed the picture before without realizing that I had noticed it, and then just fancied the face at the window."

"The end window?" said Mrs. Harter sharply.

"Yes, why?"

"Nothing," said Mrs. Harter.

But she was startled all the same. That room had been her husband's dressing-room.

That same evening, Charles again being absent, Mrs. Harter sat listening to the wireless with feverish impatience. If for the third time she heard the mysterious voice, it would prove to her finally and without a shadow of doubt that she was really in communication with some other world.

Although her heart beat faster, she was not surprised when the same break occurred, and after the usual interval of deathly silence the faint faraway Irish voice spoke once more.

"*Mary—you are prepared now. . . . On Friday I shall come for you. . . . Friday at half past nine. . . . Do not be afraid—there will be no pain. . . . Be ready. . . .*"

Then, almost cutting short the last word, the music of the orchestra broke out again, clamorous and discordant.

Mrs. Harter sat very still for a minute or two. Her face had gone white and she looked blue and pinched round the lips.

Presently she got up and sat down at her writing-desk. In a somewhat shaky hand she wrote the following lines:

Tonight, at 9:15, I have distinctly heard the voice of my dead husband. He told me that he would come for me on Friday night at 9:30. If I should die on that day and at that hour I should like the facts made known so as to prove beyond question the possibility of communicating with the spirit world.—Mary Harter.

Mrs. Harter read over what she had written, enclosed it in an envelope, and addressed the envelope. Then she rang the bell which was promptly answered by Elizabeth. Mrs. Harter got up from her desk and gave the note she had just written to the old woman.

"Elizabeth," she said, "if I should die on Friday night I should like that note given to Doctor Meynell. No"—as Elizabeth appeared about to protest—"do not argue with me. You have often told me you believe in premonitions. I have a premonition now. There is one thing more. I have left you in my will fifty pounds. I should like you to have a hundred pounds. If I am not able to go to the bank myself before I die, Mr. Charles will see to it."

As before, Mrs. Harter cut short Elizabeth's tearful protests. In pursuance of her determination the old lady spoke to her nephew on the subject the following morning.

"Remember, Charles, that if anything should happen to me, Elizabeth is to have an extra fifty pounds."

"You are very gloomy these days, Aunt Mary," said Charles cheerfully. "What is going to happen to you? According to Doctor Meynell, we shall be celebrating your hundredth birthday in twenty years or so!"

Mrs. Harter smiled affectionately at him but did not answer. After a minute or two she said, "What are you doing on Friday evening, Charles?"

Charles looked a trifle surprised.

"As a matter of fact, the Ewings asked me to go in and play bridge, but if you would rather I stayed at home—"

"No," said Mrs. Harter with determination. "Certainly not. I mean it, Charles. On that night of all nights I should much rather be alone."

Charles looked at her curiously, but Mrs. Harter vouchsafed no further information. She was an old lady of courage and determination. She felt that she must go through with her strange experience singlehanded.

Friday evening found the house very silent. Mrs. Harter sat as usual in her straight-backed chair drawn up to the fireplace. All her preparations were made. That morning she had been to the bank, had drawn out £50 in notes, and had handed them over to Elizabeth despite the latter's tearful protests. She had sorted and arranged all her personal belongings and had labeled one or two pieces of jewelry with the names of friends or relations. She had also written out a list of instructions for Charles. The Worcester tea service was to go to Cousin Emma, the Sèvres jars to young William, and so on.

Now she looked at the long envelope she held in her hand and drew from it a folded document. This was her will sent to her by Mr. Hopkinson in accordance with her instructions. She had already read it carefully, but now she looked over it once more to refresh her memory. It was a short, concise document. A bequest of £50 to Elizabeth Marshall in consideration of faithful service; two bequests of £500 to a sister and a first cousin, and the remainder to her beloved nephew Charles Ridgeway.

Mrs. Harter nodded her head several times. Charles would be a very rich man when she was dead. Well, he had been a dear good boy to her. Always kind, always affectionate, and with a merry tongue which never failed to please her.

She looked at the clock. Three minutes to the half-hour. Well, she was ready. And she was calm—quite calm. Although she repeated these last words to herself several times, her heart beat strangely and unevenly. She hardly realized it herself, but she was strung up to a fine point of overwrought nerves.

Half past nine. The wireless was switched on. What would she hear? A familiar voice announcing the weather forecast or that faraway voice belonging to a man who had died twenty-five years before?

But she heard neither. Instead there came a familiar sound, a sound she knew well but which tonight made her feel as though an icy hand were laid on her heart. A fumbling at the front door—

It came again. And then a cold blast seemed to sweep through the room. Mrs. Harter had now no doubt what her sensations were. She was afraid. She was more than afraid—she was terrified—

And suddenly there came to her the thought: *Twenty-five years is a long time. Patrick is a stranger to me now.*

Terror! That was what was invading her.

A soft step outside the door—a soft, halting footstep. Then the door swung silently open—

Mrs. Harter staggered to her feet, swaying slightly from side to side, her eyes fixed on the open doorway. Something slipped from her fingers into the grate.

She gave a strangled cry which died in her throat. In the dim light of the doorway stood a familiar figure with chestnut beard and whiskers and an old-fashioned Victorian coat.

Patrick had come for her!

Her heart gave one terrified leap and stood still. She slipped to the ground in a crumpled heap.

There Elizabeth found her, an hour later.

Dr. Meynell was called at once and Charles Ridgeway was hastily summoned from his bridge party. But nothing could be done. Mrs. Harter was beyond human aid.

It was not until two days later that Elizabeth remembered the note given to her by her mistress. Dr. Meynell read it with great interest and showed it to Charles Ridgeway.

"A very curious coincidence," he said. "It seems clear that your aunt had been having hallucinations about her dead husband's voice. She must have strung herself up to such a point that the excitement was fatal, and when the time actually came she died of the shock."

"Auto-suggestion?" asked Charles.

"Something of the sort. I will let you know the result of the autopsy as soon as possible, though I have no doubt of it myself. In the circumstances an autopsy is desirable, though purely as a matter of form."

Charles nodded comprehendingly.

On the preceding night, when the household was in bed, he had removed a certain wire which ran from the back of the radio cabinet to his bedroom on the floor above. Also, since the evening had been a chilly one, he had asked Elizabeth to light a fire in his room, and in that fire he had burned a chestnut beard and whiskers. Some Victorian clothing belonging to his late uncle he replaced in the camphor-scented chest in the attic.

As far as he could see, he was perfectly safe. His plan, the shadowy outline of which had first formed in his brain when Doctor Meynell had told him that his aunt might with due care live for many years, had succeeded admirably. A sudden shock, Dr. Meynell had said. Charles, that affectionate young man, beloved of old ladies, smiled to himself.

When the doctor had departed, Charles went about his duties mechanically. Certain funeral arrangements had to be finally settled. Relatives coming from a distance had to have trains looked out for them. In one or two cases they would have to stay the night. Charles went about it all efficiently and methodically, to the accompaniment of an undercurrent of his own thoughts.

A very good stroke of business! That was the burden of them. Nobody, least of all his dead aunt, had known in what perilous straits Charles stood. His activities, carefully concealed from the world, had landed him where the shadow of a prison loomed ahead.

Exposure and ruin had stared him in the face unless he could in a few short months raise a considerable sum of money. Well—that was all right now. Charles smiled to himself. Thanks to—yes, call it a practical joke—nothing criminal about *that*—he was saved. He was now a very rich man. He had no anxieties on the subject, for Mrs. Harter had never made any secret of her intentions.

Chiming in very appositely with these thoughts, Elizabeth put her head round the door and informed him that Mr. Hopkinson was here and would like to see him.

About time, too, Charles thought. Repressing a tendency to whistle, he composed his face to one of suitable gravity and went to the library. There he greeted the precise old gentleman who had been for over a quarter of a century the late Mrs. Harter's legal adviser.

The lawyer seated himself at Charles's invitation and with a dry little cough entered upon business matters.

"I did not quite understand your letter to me, Mr. Ridgeway. You seemed to be under the impression that the late Mrs. Harter's will was in our keeping."

Charles stared at him.

"But surely—I've heard my aunt say as much."

"Oh! quite so, quite so. It *was* in our keeping."

"*Was?*"

"That is what I said. Mrs. Harter wrote to us, asking that it might be forwarded to her on Tuesday last."

An uneasy feeling crept over Charles. He felt a far-off premonition of unpleasantness.

"Doubtless it will come to light among her papers," continued the lawyer smoothly.

Charles said nothing. He was afraid to trust his tongue. He had already been through Mrs. Harter's papers pretty thoroughly, well enough to be quite certain that no will was among them. In a minute or two, when he had regained control of himself, he said so. His voice sounded unreal to himself, and he had a sensation as of cold water trickling down his back.

"Has anyone been through her personal effects?" asked the lawyer.

Charles replied that the maid, Elizabeth, had done so. At Mr. Hopkinson's suggestion Elizabeth was sent for. She came promptly, grim and upright, and answered the questions put to her.

She had been through all her mistress's clothes and personal belongings. She was quite sure that there had been no legal document such as a will among them. She knew what the will looked like—her poor mistress had had it in her hand only the morning of her death.

"You are sure of that?" asked the lawyer sharply.

"Yes, sir. She told me so. And she made me take fifty pounds in notes. The will was in a long blue envelope."

"Quite right," said Mr. Hopkinson.

"Now I come to think of it," continued Elizabeth, "that same blue envelope was lying on this table the morning after—but empty. I laid it on the desk."

"I remember seeing it there," said Charles.

He got up and went over to the desk. In a minute or two he turned round with an envelope in his hand which he handed to Mr. Hopkinson. The latter examined it and nodded his head.

"That is the envelope in which I dispatched the will on Tuesday last."

Both men looked hard at Elizabeth.

"Is there anything more, sir?" she inquired respectfully.

"Not at present, thank you."

Elizabeth went toward the door.

"One minute," said the lawyer. "Was there a fire in the grate that evening?"

"Yes, sir, there was always a fire."

"Thank you, that will do."

Elizabeth went out. Charles leaned forward, resting a shaking hand on the table.

"What do you think? What are you driving at?"

Mr. Hopkinson shook his head.

"We must still hope the will may turn up. If it does not—"

"Well, if it does not?"

"I am afraid there is only one conclusion possible. Your aunt sent for that will in order to destroy it. Not wishing Elizabeth to lose by that, she gave her the amount of her legacy in cash."

"But why?" cried Charles wildly. "Why?"

Mr. Hopkinson coughed. A dry cough.

"You have had no—er—disagreement with your aunt, Mr. Ridgeway?" he murmured.

Charles gasped.

"No, indeed," he cried warmly. "We were on the kind-liest, most affectionate terms, right up to the end."

"Ah!" said Mr. Hopkinson, not looking at him.

It came to Charles with a shock that the lawyer did not believe him. Who knew what this dry old stick might not have heard? Rumors of Charles's doings might have come round to him. What more natural than that he should suppose that these same rumors had come to Mrs. Harter, and that aunt and nephew should have had an altercation on the subject?

But it wasn't so! Charles knew one of the bitterest moments of his career. His lies had been believed. Now that he spoke the truth, belief was withheld. The irony of it!

Of course his aunt had never burned the will! Of course—

His thoughts came to a sudden check. What was that picture rising before his eyes? An old lady with one hand clasped to her heart—something slipping—a paper—falling on the red-hot embers—

Charles's face grew livid. He heard a hoarse voice—his own—asking, "If that will's never found?"

"There is a former will of Mrs. Harter's still extant. Dated September, 1920. By it Mrs. Harter leaves everything to her niece, Miriam Harter, now Miriam Robinson."

What was the old fool saying? Miriam? Miriam with her nondescript husband, and her four whining brats. All his cleverness—for Miriam!

The telephone rang sharply at his elbow. He took up the receiver. It was the doctor's voice, hearty and kindly.

"That you, Ridgeway? Thought you'd like to know. The autopsy's just concluded. Cause of death as I surmised. But as a matter of fact the cardiac trouble was much more serious than I suspected when she was alive. With the utmost care she couldn't have lived longer than two months at the outside. Thought you'd like to know. Might console you more or less."

"Excuse me," said Charles, "would you mind saying that again?"

"She couldn't have lived longer than two months," said the doctor in a slightly louder tone. "All things work out for the best, you know, my dear fellow—"

But Charles had slammed back the receiver on its hook. He was conscious of the lawyer's voice speaking from a long way off.

"Dear me, Mr. Ridgeway, are you ill?"

Damn them all! The smug-faced lawyer. That poisonous old ass Meynell. No hope in front of him—only the shadow of the prison wall.

He felt that Somebody had been playing with him—playing with him like a cat with a mouse. Somebody must be laughing. . . .

THE MYSTERY OF THE BLUE JAR

JACK HARTINGTON surveyed his topped drive ruefully. Standing by the ball, he looked back to the tee, measuring the distance. His face was eloquent of the disgusted contempt which he felt. With a sigh he drew out his iron, executed two vicious swings with it, annihilating in turn a dandelion and a tuft of grass, and then addressed himself firmly to the ball.

It is hard when you are twenty-four years of age, and your one ambition in life is to reduce your handicap at golf, to be forced to give time and attention to the problem of earning your living. Five and a half days out of the seven saw Jack imprisoned in a kind of mahogany tomb in the city. Saturday afternoon and Sunday were religiously devoted to the real business of life, and in an excess of zeal he had taken rooms at the small hotel near Stourton Heath links, and rose daily at the hour of six a.m. to get in an hour's practice before catching the 8:46 to town.

The only disadvantage to the plan was that he seemed constitutionally unable to hit anything at that hour in the morning. A foozled iron succeeded a muffed drive. His mashie shots ran merrily along the ground, and four putts seemed to be the minimum on any green.

Jack sighed, grasped his iron firmly, and repeated to himself the magic words, *Left arm right through, and don't look up*.

He swung back—and then stopped, petrified, as a shrill cry rent the silence of the summer's morning.

"Murder," it called. "Help! Murder!"

It was a woman's voice, and it died away at the end into a sort of gurgling sigh.

Jack flung down his club and ran in the direction of the

sound. It had come from somewhere quite near at hand. This particular part of the course was quite wild country, and there were few houses about. In fact, there was only one near at hand, a small picturesque cottage, which Jack had often noticed for its air of Old World daintiness. It was toward this cottage that he ran. It was hidden from him by a heather-covered slope, but he rounded this and in less than a minute was standing with his hand on the small latched gate.

There was a girl standing in the garden, and for a moment Jack jumped to the natural conclusion that it was she who had uttered the cry for help. But he quickly changed his mind.

She had a little basket in her hand, half full of weeds, and had evidently just straightened herself up from weeding a wide border of pansies. Her eyes, Jack noticed, were just like pansies themselves, velvety and soft and dark, and more violet than blue. She was like a pansy altogether, in her straight purple linen gown.

The girl was looking at Jack with an expression midway between annoyance and surprise.

"I beg your pardon," said the young man. "But did you cry out just now?"

"I? No, indeed."

Her surprise was so genuine that Jack felt confused. Her voice was very soft and pretty with a slight foreign inflection.

"But you must have heard it," he exclaimed. "It came from somewhere just near here."

She stared at him. "I heard nothing at all."

Jack in his turn stared at her. It was perfectly incredible that she should not have heard that agonized appeal for help. And yet her calmness was so evident that he could not believe she was lying to him.

"It came from somewhere close at hand," he insisted.

She was looking at him suspiciously now.

"What did it say?" she asked.

"Murder—help! Murder!"

"Murder—help, murder," repeated the girl. "Somebody has played a trick on you, monsieur. Who could be murdered here?"

Jack looked about him with a confused idea of discovering a dead body upon a garden path. Yet he was still perfectly sure that the cry he had heard was real and not a product of his imagination. He looked up at the cottage windows. Everything seemed perfectly still and peaceful.

"Do you want to search our house?" asked the girl dryly.

She was so clearly skeptical that Jack's confusion grew deeper than ever. He turned away.

"I'm sorry," he said. "It must have come from higher up in the woods."

He raised his cap and retreated. Glancing back over his shoulder, he saw that the girl had calmly resumed her weeding.

For some time he hunted through the woods, but could find no sign of anything unusual having occurred. Yet he was as positive as ever that he had really heard the cry. In the end, he gave up the search and hurried home to bolt his breakfast and catch the 8:46 by the usual narrow margin of a second or so. His conscience pricked him a little as he sat in the train. Ought he not to have immediately reported what he had heard to the police? That he had not done so was solely owing to the pansy girl's incredulity. She had clearly suspected him of romancing—possibly the police might do the same. Was he absolutely certain that he had heard the cry?

By now he was not nearly so positive as he had been—the natural result of trying to recapture a lost sensation. Was it some bird's cry in the distance that he had twisted into the resemblance of a woman's voice?

But he rejected the suggestion angrily. It was a woman's voice, and he had heard it. He remembered looking at his watch just before the cry had come. As nearly as possible it must have been five and twenty minutes past seven when he had heard the call. That might be a fact useful to the police if—if anything should be discovered.

Going home that evening, he scanned the evening papers anxiously to see if there were any mention of a crime having been committed. But there was nothing, and he hardly knew whether to be relieved or disappointed.

The following morning was wet—so wet that even the most ardent golfer might have his enthusiasm damped. Jack rose at the last possible moment, gulped his breakfast, ran for the train, and again eagerly scanned the papers. Still no mention of any gruesome discovery having been made. The evening papers told the same tale.

Queer, said Jack to himself, *but there it is. Probably some blinking little boys having a game together up in the woods.*

He was out early the following morning. As he passed the cottage, he noted out of the tail of his eye that the girl was out in the garden again weeding. Evidently a habit of hers. He did a particularly good approach shot, and hoped that she had noticed it. As he teed up on the next tee, he glanced at his watch.

"Just five and twenty past seven," he murmured. "I wonder—"

The words were frozen on his lips. From behind him came the same cry which had so startled him before. A woman's voice, in dire distress.

"Murder—help, murder!"

Jack raced back. The pansy girl was standing by the gate. She looked startled, and Jack ran up to her triumphantly, crying out, "You heard it this time, anyway."

Her eyes were wide with some emotion he could not fathom but he noticed that she shrank back from him as he approached, and even glanced back at the house, as though she meditated running to it for shelter.

She shook her head, staring at him.

"I heard nothing at all," she said wonderingly.

It was as though she had struck him a blow between the eyes. Her sincerity was so evident that he could not disbelieve her. Yet he couldn't have imagined it—he couldn't —he couldn't— He heard her voice speaking gently—almost with sympathy.

"You have had the shell-shock, yes?"

In a flash he understood her look of fear, her glance back at the house. She thought that he suffered from delusions.

And then, like a douche of cold water, came the horrible thought, was she right? Did he suffer from delusions? Obsessed by the horror of the thought, he turned and stumbled away without vouchsafing a word. The girl watched him go, sighed, shook her head, and bent down to her weeding again.

Jack endeavored to reason matters out with himself. *If I hear the damned thing again at twenty-five minutes past seven,* he said to himself, *it's clear that I've got hold of a hallucination of some sort. But I won't hear it.*

He was nervous all day, and went to bed early, determined to put the matter to the proof the following morning.

As was perhaps natural in such a case, he remained awake half the night and finally overslept himself. It was twenty past seven by the time he was clear of the hotel and running toward the links. He realized that he would not be able to get to the fatal spot by twenty-five past, but surely, if the voice were a hallucination pure and simple, he would hear it anywhere. He ran on, his eyes fixed on the hands of his watch.

Twenty-five past. From far off came the echo of a woman's voice, calling. The words could not be distinguished, but he was convinced that it was the same cry he had heard before, and that it came from the same spot, somewhere in the neighborhood of the cottage.

Strangely enough, that fact reassured him. It might, after all, be a hoax. Unlikely as it seemed, the girl herself might be playing a trick on him. He set his shoulders resolutely, and took out a club from his golf bag. He would play the few holes up to the cottage.

The girl was in the garden as usual. She looked up this morning, and when he raised his cap to her, said good-morning rather shyly. She looked, he thought, lovelier than ever.

"Nice day, isn't it?" Jack called out cheerily, cursing the unavoidable banality of the observation.

"Yes, indeed, it is lovely."

"Good for the garden, I expect?"

The girl smiled a little, disclosing a fascinating dimple.

"Alas, no! For my flowers the rain is needed. See, they are all dried up."

Jack accepted the invitation of her gesture, and came up to the low hedge dividing the garden from the course, looking over it into the garden.

"They seem all right," he remarked awkwardly, conscious as he spoke of the girl's slightly pitying glance running over him.

"The sun is good, is it not?" she said. "For the flowers one can always water them. But the sun gives strength and repairs the health. Monsieur is much better today, I can see."

Her encouraging tone annoyed Jack intensely. *Curse it all,* he said to himself. *I believe she's trying to cure me by suggestion.*

"I'm perfectly well," he said irritably.

"That is good, then," returned the girl, quickly and soothingly.

Jack had the irritating feeling that she didn't believe him.

He played a few more holes and hurried back to breakfast. As he ate it, he was conscious, not for the first time, of the close scrutiny of a man who sat at the table next to him. He was a man of middle age, with a powerful, forceful face. He had a small dark beard and very piercing gray eyes, and an ease and assurance of manner which placed him among the higher ranks of the professional classes. His name, Jack knew, was Lavington, and he had heard vague rumors as to his being a well-known medical specialist, but as Jack was not a frequenter of Harley Street, the name had conveyed little or nothing to him.

But this morning he was very conscious of the quiet observation under which he was being kept, and it frightened him a little. Was his secret written plainly in his face for all to see? Did this man, by reason of his professional calling, know that there was something amiss in the hidden gray matter?

Jack shivered at the thought. Was it true? Was he really going mad? Was the whole thing a hallucination, or was it a gigantic hoax?

And suddenly a very simple way of testing the solution occurred to him. He had hitherto been alone on his round. Supposing someone else was with him? Then one out of three things might happen. The voice might be silent. They might both hear it. Or—he only might hear it.

That evening he proceeded to carry his plan into effect. Lavington was the man he wanted with him. They fell into conversation easily enough—the older man might have been waiting for such an opening. It was clear that for some reason or other Jack interested him. The latter was able to come quite easily and naturally to the suggestion that they might play a few holes together before breakfast. The arrangement was made for the following morning.

They started out a little before seven. It was a perfect day, still and cloudless, but not too warm. The doctor was playing well, Jack wretchedly. His whole mind was intent on the forthcoming crisis. He kept glancing surreptitiously at his watch. They reached the seventh tee, between which and the hole the cottage was situated, about twenty past seven.

The girl, as usual, was in the garden as they passed. She did not look up as they passed.

The two balls lay on the green, Jack's near the hole, the doctor's some little distance away.

"I've got this for it," said Lavington. "I must go for it, I suppose."

He bent down, judging the line he should take. Jack stood rigid, his eyes glued on his watch. It was exactly twenty-five minutes past seven.

The ball ran swiftly along the grass, stopped on the edge of the hole, hesitated, and dropped in.

"Good putt," said Jack. His voice sounded hoarse and unlike himself. He shoved his wrist watch farther up his arm with a sigh of overwhelming relief. Nothing had happened. The spell was broken.

"If you don't mind waiting a minute," he said, "I think I'll have a pipe."

They paused a while on the eighth tee. Jack filled and lit the pipe with fingers that trembled a little in spite of himself. An enormous weight seemed to have lifted from his mind.

"Lord, what a good day it is," he remarked, staring at the prospect ahead of him with great contentment. "Go on, Lavington, your swipe."

And then it came. Just at the very instant the doctor was hitting. A woman's voice, high and agonized.

"Murder— Help! Murder!"

The pipe fell from Jack's nerveless hand as he spun round in the direction of the sound and then, remembering, gazed breathlessly at his companion.

Lavington was looking down the course, shading his eyes.

"A bit short—just cleared the bunker, though, I think."

He had heard nothing.

The world seemed to spin round with Jack. He took a step or two, lurching heavily. When he recovered himself, he was lying on the short turf and Lavington was bending over him.

"There, take it easy now, take it easy."

"What did I do?"

"You fainted, young man—or gave a very good try at it."

"My God!" said Jack, and groaned.

"What's the trouble? Something on your mind?"

"I'll tell you in one minute, but I'd like to ask you something first."

The doctor lit his own pipe and settled himself on the bank. "Ask anything you like," he said comfortably.

"You've been watching me for the last day or two. Why?"

Lavington's eyes twinkled a little.

"That's rather an awkward question. A cat can look at a king, you know."

"Don't put me off. I'm in earnest. Why was it? I've a vital reason for asking."

Lavington's face grew serious.

"I'll answer you quite honestly. I recognized in you all the signs of a man laboring under a sense of acute strain, and it intrigued me what that strain could be."

"I can tell you that easily enough," said Jack bitterly. "I'm going mad."

He stopped dramatically, but his statement not seeming to arouse the interest and consternation he expected, he repeated it.

"I tell you I'm going mad."

"Very curious," murmured Lavington. "Very curious indeed."

Jack felt indignant.

"I suppose that's all it does seem to you. Doctors are so damned callous."

"Come, come, my young friend, you're talking at random. To begin with, although I have taken my degree, I do not practice medicine. Strictly speaking, I am not a doctor—not a doctor of the body, that is."

Jack looked at him keenly.

"Of the mind?"

"Yes, in a sense, but more truly I call myself a doctor of the soul."

"Oh!"

"I perceive the disparagement in your tone, and yet we must use some word to denote the active principle which can be separated and exist independently of its fleshy home, the body. You've got to come to terms with the soul, you know, young man; it isn't just a religious term invented by clergymen. But we'll call it the mind, or the subconscious self, or any term that suits you better. You took offense at my tone just now, but I can assure you that it really did strike me as very curious that such a well-balanced and perfectly normal young man as yourself should suffer from the delusion that he was going out of his mind."

"I'm out of my mind, all right. Absolutely balmy."

"You will forgive me for saying so, but I don't believe it."

"I suffer from delusions."

"After dinner?"

"No, in the morning."

"Can't be done," said the doctor, relighting his pipe which had gone out.

"I tell you I hear things that no one else hears."

"One man in a thousand can see the moons of Jupiter. Because the other nine hundred and ninety-nine can't see them there's no reason to doubt that the moons of Jupiter exist, and certainly no reason for calling the thousandth man a lunatic."

"The moons of Jupiter are a proved scientific fact."

"It's quite possible that the delusions of today may be

the proved scientific facts of tomorrow."

In spite of himself, Lavington's matter-of-fact manner was having its effect upon Jack. He felt immeasurably soothed and cheered. The doctor looked at him attentively for a minute or two and then nodded.

"That's better," he said. "The trouble with you young fellows is that you're so cocksure nothing can exist outside your own philosophy that you get the wind up when something occurs to jolt you out of that opinion. Let's hear your grounds for believing that you're going mad, and we'll decide whether or not to lock you up afterward."

As faithfully as he could, Jack narrated the whole series of occurrences.

"But what I can't understand," he ended, "is why this morning it should come at half past seven—five minutes late."

Lavington thought for a minute or two. Then—

"What's the time now by your watch?" he asked.

"Quarter to eight," replied Jack, consulting it.

"That's simple enough, then. Mine says twenty to eight. Your watch is five minutes fast. That's a very interesting and important point—to me. In fact, it's invaluable."

"In what way?"

Jack was beginning to get interested.

"Well, the obvious explanation is that on the first morning you *did* hear some such cry—may have been a joke, may not. On the following mornings, you suggestioned yourself to hear it exactly the same time."

"I'm sure I didn't."

"Not consciously, of course, but the subconscious plays us some funny tricks, you know. But, anyway, that explanation won't wash. If it were a case of suggestion, you would have heard the cry at twenty-five minutes past seven by your watch, and you could never have heard it when the time, as you thought, was past."

"Well, then?"

link in the chain came from an unexpected
getting back one day, Jack was informed that
y was waiting to see him. To his intense sur-
ed to be the girl of the garden—the pansy girl,
s called her in his own mind. She was very
confused.

forgive me, monsieur, for coming to seek you
t there is something I want to tell you—I—"
l around uncertainly.

here," said Jack promptly, leading the way
deserted ladies' drawing-room of the hotel,
rtment, with a good deal of red plush about
down, Miss—Miss—"

, monsieur. Felise Marchaud."

Mademoiselle Marchaud, and tell me all

lown obediently. She was dressed in dark
nd the beauty and charm of the proud little
evident than ever. Jack's heart beat faster as
eside her.

his," explained Felise. "We have been here
ime, and from the beginning we hear the
sweet little house—is haunted. No servant
That does not matter so much—me, I can
and cook easily enough."

ght the infatuated young man. *She's won-*
maintained an outward semblance of busi-
ion.

f ghosts, I think it is all folly—that is until
Monsieur, four nights running, I have had
. A lady stands there—she is beautiful, tall,
In her hands she holds a blue china jar.
—very distressed, and continually she holds
e, as though imploring me to do something
s! She cannot speak, and I—I do not know
That was the dream for the first two nights

"Well—it's obvious, isn't it? This cry for help occupies a
perfectly definite place and time in space. The place is
the vicinity of that cottage and the time is twenty-five minutes past seven."

"Yes, but why should I be the one to hear it? I don't believe in ghosts and all that spook stuff—spirits rapping and
all the rest of it. Why should I hear the damned thing?"

"Ah! That we can't tell at present. It's a curious thing
that many of the best mediums are made out of confirmed
skeptics. It isn't the people who are interested in occult
phenomena who get the manifestations. Some people see
and hear things that other people don't—we don't know
why, and nine times out of ten they don't want to see or
hear them, and are convinced that they are suffering from
delusions—just as you were. It's like electricity. Some substances are good conductors, and for a long time we didn't
know why, and had to be content just to accept the fact.
Nowadays we do know why. Some day, no doubt, we shall
know why you hear this thing and I and the girl don't.
Everything's governed by natural law, you know—there's
no such thing really as the supernatural. Finding out the
laws that govern so-called psychic phenomena is going to
be a tough job—but every little helps."

"But what am I going to do?" asked Jack.

Lavington chuckled.

"Practical, I see. Well, my young friend, you are going to
have a good breakfast and get off to the city without worrying your head further about things you don't understand.
I, on the other hand, am going to poke about, and see
what I can find out about that cottage back there. That's
where the mystery centers, I dare swear."

Jack rose to his feet.

"Right, sir. I'm on, but, I say—"

"Yes?"

Jack flushed awkwardly.

"I'm sure the girl's all right," he muttered.

Lavington looked amused.

"You didn't tell me she was a pretty girl! Well, cheer up, I think the mystery started before her time."

Jack arrived home that evening in a perfect fever of curiosity. He was by now pinning his faith blindly to Lavington. The doctor had accepted the matter so naturally, had been so matter-of-fact and unperturbed by it, that Jack was impressed.

He found his new friend waiting for him in the hall when he came down for dinner, and the doctor suggested that they should dine together at the same table.

"Any news, sir?" asked Jack anxiously.

"I've collected the life history of Heather Cottage all right. It was tenanted first by an old gardener and his wife. The old man died, and the old woman went to her daughter. Then a builder got hold of it, and modernized it with great success, selling it to a city gentleman who used it for week-ends. About a year ago, he sold it to some people called Turner—Mr. and Mrs. Turner. They seem to have been rather a curious couple from all I can make out. He was an Englishman, his wife was popularly supposed to be partly Russian, and was a very handsome, exotic-looking woman. They lived very quietly, seeing no one, and hardly ever going outside the cottage garden. The local rumor goes that they were afraid of something—but I don't think we ought to rely on that.

"And then suddenly one day they departed, cleared out one morning early, and never came back. The agents here got a letter from Mr. Turner, written from London, instructing him to sell the place as quickly as possible. The furniture was sold off, and the house itself was sold to a Mr. Mauleverer. He only actually lived in it a fortnight— then he advertised it to be let furnished. The people who have it now are a consumptive French professor and his daughter. They have been there just ten days."

Jack digested this in silence.

"I don't see that that gets u
last. "Do you?"

"I rather want to know mor
Lavington quietly. "They left
you remember. As far as I can
saw them go. Mr. Turner has
find anybody who has seen M

Jack paled.

"It can't be—you don't mea

"Don't excite yourself, you
anyone at the point of deat
death—upon their surroundin
roundings might conceival
transmitting it in turn to a su
case yourself."

"But why me?" murmured
someone who could do some

"You are regarding the for
ful, instead of blind and me
self in earth-bound spirits, h
ular purpose. But the thing
until I can hardly believe i
kind of blind groping towar
ing of blind forces, always v
end—"

He shook himself—as tho
that preoccupied him, and
smile.

"Let us banish the subjec
suggested.

Jack agreed readily enou
to banish the subject from

During the week-end, he
own, but succeeded in elici
had done. He had definite
breakfast.

The nex
quarter. O
a young la
prise it pr
as he alwa
nervous an

"You wi
like this?

She look

"Come i
into the ne
a dreary ap
it. "Now, s

"Marcha

"Sit dow
about it."

Felise sa
green today
face was mo
he sat down

"It is like
but a shor
house—our
will stay in
do the mén
Angel, th
derful. But
nesslike atte

"This tall
four days ag
the same dre
and very fa
She is distres
out the jar t
with it. But
what she ask

—but the night before last, there was more of it. She and the blue jar faded away, and suddenly I heard her voice crying out—I know it is her voice, you comprehend—and, oh! Monsieur, the words she says are those you spoke to me that morning. 'Murder—help! Murder!' I awake in terror. I say to myself—it is a nightmare, the words you heard are an accident. But last night the dream came again. Monsieur, what is it? You, too, have heard. What shall we do?"

Felise's face was terrified. Her small hands clasped themselves together, and she gazed appealingly at Jack. The latter affected an unconcern he did not feel.

"That's all right, Mademoiselle Marchaud. You mustn't worry. I tell you what I'd like you to do, if you don't mind. Repeat the whole story to a friend of mine who is staying here, a Doctor Lavington."

Felise signified her willingness to adopt this course, and Jack went off in search of Lavington. He returned with him a few minutes later.

Lavington gave the girl a keen scrutiny as he acknowledged Jack's hurried introductions. With a few reassuring words, he soon put the girl at her ease, and he, in his turn, listened attentively to her story.

"Very curious," he said when she had finished. "You have told your father this?"

Felise shook her head.

"I have not liked to worry him. He is very ill still"—her eyes filled with tears—"I keep from him anything that might excite or agitate him."

"I understand," said Lavington kindly. "And I am glad you came to us, Mademoiselle Marchaud. Hartington here, as you know, had an experience something similar to yours. I think I may say that we are well on the track now. There is nothing else that you can think of?"

Felise gave a quick movement.

"Of course! How stupid I am. It is the point of the whole

story. Look, monsieur, at what I found at the back of one of the cupboards where it had slipped behind the shelf."

She held out to them a dirty piece of drawing-paper on which was executed roughly in water colors a sketch of a woman. It was a mere daub, but the likeness was probably good enough. It represented a tall, fair woman, with something subtly un-English in her face. She was standing by a table on which was standing a blue china jar.

"I only found it this morning," explained Felise. *"Monsieur le docteur,* that is the face of the woman I saw in my dream, and that is the identical blue jar."

"Extraordinary," commented Lavington. "The key to the mystery is evidently the blue jar. It looks like a Chinese jar to me, probably an old one. It seems to have a curious raised pattern over it."

"It is Chinese," declared Jack. "I have seen an exactly similar one in my uncle's collection—he is a great collector of Chinese porcelain, you know, and I remember noticing a jar just like this a short time ago."

"The Chinese jar," mused Lavington. He remained a minute or two lost in thought, then raised his head suddenly, a curious light shining in his eyes. "Hartington, how long has your uncle had that jar?"

"How long? I really don't know."

"Think. Did he buy it lately?"

"I don't know—yes, I believe he did, now I come to think of it. I'm not very interested in porcelain myself, but I remember his showing me his 'recent acquisitions,' and this was one of them."

"Less than two months ago? The Turners left Heather Cottage just two months ago."

"Yes, I believe it was."

"Your uncle attends country sales sometimes?"

"He's always tooling round to sales."

"Then there is no inherent improbability in our assuming that he bought this particular piece of porcelain at the sale of the Turners' things. A curious coincidence—or perhaps what I call the groping of blind justice. Hartington, you must find out from your uncle at once where he bought this jar."

Jack's face fell.

"I'm afraid that's impossible. Uncle George is away on the Continent. I don't even know where to write to him."

"How long will he be away?"

"Three weeks to a month at least."

There was a silence. Felise sat looking anxiously from one man to the other.

"Is there nothing that we can do?" she asked timidly.

"Yes, there is one thing," said Lavington, in a tone of suppressed excitement. "It is unusual, perhaps, but I believe that it will succeed. Hartington, you must get hold of that jar. Bring it down here and, if mademoiselle permits, we will spend a night in Heather Cottage, taking the blue jar with us."

Jack felt his skin creep uncomfortably. "What do you think will happen?" he asked uneasily.

"I have not the slightest idea—but I honestly believe that the mystery will be solved and the ghost laid. Quite possibly there may be a false bottom to the jar and something is concealed inside. If no phenomenon occurs, we must use our own ingenuity."

Felise clasped her hands. "It is a wonderful idea," she exclaimed.

Her eyes were alight with enthusiasm. Jack did not feel nearly so enthusiastic—in fact, he was inwardly funking it badly, but nothing would have induced him to admit the fact before Felise. The doctor acted as though his suggestion were the most natural one in the world.

"When can you get the jar?" asked Felise, turning to Jack.

"Tomorrow," said the latter, unwillingly.

He had to go through with it now, but the memory of

that frenzied cry for help that had haunted him each morning was something to be ruthlessly thrust down and not thought about more than could be helped.

He went to his uncle's house the following evening, and took away the jar in question. He was more than ever convinced when he saw it again that it was the identical one pictured in the water-color sketch, but carefully as he looked it over he could see no sign that it contained a secret receptacle of any kind.

It was eleven o'clock when he and Lavington arrived at Heather Cottage. Felise was on the lookout for them, and opened the door softly before they had time to knock.

"Come in," she whispered. "My father is asleep upstairs, and we must not wake him. I have made coffee for you in here."

She led the way into a small cozy sitting-room. A spirit lamp stood in the grate, and bending over it, she brewed them both some fragrant coffee.

Then Jack unfastened the Chinese jar from its many wrappings. Felise gasped as her eyes fell on it.

"But yes, but yes," she cried eagerly. "That is it—I would know it anywhere."

Meanwhile Lavington was making his own preparations. He removed all the ornaments from a small table and set it in the middle of the room. Round it he placed three chairs. Then, taking the blue jar from Jack, he placed it in the center of the table.

"Now," he said, "we are ready. Turn off the lights, and let us sit round the table in the darkness."

The others obeyed him. Lavington's voice spoke again out of the darkness.

"Think of nothing—or of everything. Do not force the mind. It is possible that one of us has mediumistic powers. If so, that person will go into a trance. Remember, there is nothing to fear. Cast out fear from your hearts, and drift— drift—"

His voice died away and there was silence. Minute by minute, the silence seemed to grow more pregnant with possibilities. It was all very well for Lavington to say, "Cast out fear." It was not fear that Jack felt—it was panic. And he was almost certain that Felise felt the same way. Suddenly he heard her voice, low and terrified.

"Something terrible is going to happen. I feel it."

"Cast out fear," said Lavington. "Do not fight against the influence."

The darkness seemed to get darker and the silence more acute. And nearer and nearer came that indefinable sense of menace.

Jack felt himself choking—stifling—the evil thing was very near—

And then the moment of conflict passed. He was drifting—drifting downstream—his lids closed—peace—darkness. . . .

Jack stirred slightly. His head was heavy—heavy as lead. Where was he?

Sunshine—birds— He lay staring up at the sky.

Then it all came back to him. The sitting. The little room. Felise and the doctor. What had happened?

He sat up, his head throbbing unpleasantly, and looked round him. He was lying in a little copse not far from the cottage. No one else was near him. He took out his watch. To his amazement it registered half past twelve.

Jack struggled to his feet, and ran as fast as he could in the direction of the cottage. They must have been alarmed by his failure to come out of the trance, and carried him out into the open air.

Arrived at the cottage, he knocked loudly on the door. But there was no answer, and no signs of life about it. They must have gone off to get help. Or else—Jack felt an indefinable fear invade him. What had happened last night?

He made his way back to the hotel as quickly as possible. He was about to make some inquiries at the office, when he was diverted by a colossal punch in the ribs which nearly knocked him off his feet. Turning in some indignation, he beheld a white-haired old gentleman wheezing with mirth.

"Didn't expect me, my boy. Didn't expect me, hey?" said this individual.

"Why, Uncle George, I thought you were miles away—in Italy somewhere."

"Ah! but I wasn't. Landed at Dover last night. Thought I'd motor up to town and stop here to see you on the way. And what did I find. Out all night, hey? Nice goings on—"

"Uncle George," Jack checked him firmly. "I've got the most extraordinary story to tell you. I dare say you won't believe it."

He narrated the whole story.

"And God knows what's become of them," he ended.

His uncle seemed on the verge of apoplexy. "The jar," he managed to ejaculate at last. "*The blue jar!* What's become of that?"

Jack stared at him in non-comprehension, but submerged in the torrent of words that followed he began to understand.

It came with a rush: "Ming—unique—gem of my collection—worth ten thousand pounds at least—offer from Hoggenheimer, the American millionaire—only one of its kind in the world.—Confound it, sir, what have you done with my *blue jar?*"

Jack rushed to the office. He must find Lavington. The young lady in the office eyed him coldly.

"Doctor Lavington left late last night—by motor. He left a note for you."

Jack tore it open. It was short and to the point.

My dear young friend:
Is the day of the supernatural over? Not quite—especially

when tricked out in new scientific language. Kindest regards from Felise, invalid father, and myself. We have twelve hours start, which ought to be ample.

Yours ever,
Ambrose Lavington
Doctor of the Soul.

PHILOMEL COTTAGE

"Good-by, darling."

"Good-by, sweetheart."

Alix Martin stood leaning over the small rustic gate, watching the retreating figure of her husband, as he walked down the road in the direction of the village.

Presently he turned a bend and was lost to sight, but Alix still stayed in the same position, absent-mindedly smoothing a lock of the rich brown hair which had blown across her face, her eyes faraway and dreamy.

Alix Martin was not beautiful, nor even, strictly speaking, pretty. But her face, the face of a woman no longer in her first youth, was irradiated and softened until her former colleagues of the old office days would hardly have recognized her. Miss Alix King had been a trim businesslike young woman, efficient, slightly brusque in manner, obviously capable and matter-of-fact. She had made the least, not the most, of her beautiful brown hair. Her mouth, not ungenerous in its lines, had always been severely compressed. Her clothes had been neat and suitable, without a hint of coquetry.

Alix had graduated in a hard school. For fifteen years, from the age of eighteen until she was thirty-three, she had kept herself (and for seven years of the time, an invalid mother) by her work as a shorthand-typist. It was the struggle for existence which had hardened the soft lines of her girlish face.

True, there had been romance—of a kind. Dick Windyford, a fellow clerk. Very much of a woman at heart, Alix had always known without seeming to know that he cared. Outwardly they had been friends, nothing more. Out of his slender salary, Dick had been hard put to it to provide for the schooling of a younger brother. For the moment, he could not think of marriage. Nevertheless, when Alix envisaged the future, it was with the half acknowledged certainty that she would one day be Dick's wife. They cared for one another, so she would have put it, but they were both sensible people. Plenty of time, no need to do anything rash. So the years had gone on.

And then suddenly deliverance from daily toil had come to the girl in the most unexpected manner. A distant cousin had died leaving her money to Alix. A few thousand pounds, enough to bring in a couple of hundred a year. To Alix, it was freedom, life, independence. Now she and Dick need wait no longer.

But Dick reacted unexpectedly. He had never directly spoken of his love to Alix, now he seemed less inclined to do so than ever. He avoided her, became morose and gloomy. Alix was quick to realize the truth. She had become a woman of means. Delicacy and pride stood in the way of Dick's asking her to be his wife.

She liked him none the worse for it and was indeed deliberating as to whether she herself might not take the first step when for the second time the unexpected descended upon her.

She met Gerald Martin at a friend's house. He fell violently in love with her and within a week they were engaged. Alix, who had always considered herself "not the falling-in-love kind," was swept clean off her feet.

Unwittingly she had found the way to arouse her former lover. Dick Windyford had come to her stammering with rage and anger.

"The man's a perfect stranger to you. You know nothing about him."

"I know that I love him."

"How can you know—in a week?"

"It doesn't take everyone eleven years to find out that they're in love with a girl," cried Alix angrily.

His face went white.

"I've cared for you ever since I met you. I thought that you cared, also."

Alix was truthful.

"I thought so, too," she admitted. "But that was because I didn't know what love was."

Then Dick had burst out again. Prayers, entreaties, even threats. Threats against the man who had supplanted him. It was amazing to Alix to see the volcano that existed beneath the reserved exterior of the man she thought she knew so well. Also, it frightened her a little. Dick, of course, couldn't possibly mean the things he was saying, the threats of vengeance against Gerald Martin. He was angry, that was all.

Her thoughts had gone back to that interview now, on this sunny morning, as she leaned on the gate of the cottage. She had been married a month, and she was idyllically happy. Yet, in the momentary absence of the husband who was everything to her, a tinge of anxiety invaded her perfect happiness, and the cause of that anxiety was Dick Windyford.

Three times since her marriage she had dreamed the same dream. The environment differed, but the main facts were always the same. She saw her husband lying dead and Dick Windyford standing over him, and she knew clearly and distinctly that his was the hand which had dealt the fatal blow.

But horrible though that was, there was something more horrible still—horrible that was, on awakening, for in the dream it seemed perfectly natural and inevitable. *She, Alix Martin, was glad that her husband was dead*—she stretched out grateful hands to the murderer, sometimes she thanked him. The dream always ended the same way, with herself clasped in Dick Windyford's arms.

She had said nothing of this dream to her husband, but secretly it had perturbed her more than she liked to admit.

Was it a warning—a warning against Dick Windyford? Had he some secret power which he was trying to establish over her at a distance? She did not know much about hypnotism, but surely she had always heard that persons could not be hypnotized against their will.

Alix was roused from her thoughts by the sharp ringing of the telephone bell from within the house. She entered the cottage and picked up the receiver. Suddenly she swayed, and put out a hand to keep herself from falling.

"Who did you say was speaking?"

"Why, Alix, what's the matter with your voice? I wouldn't have known it. It's Dick."

"Oh!" said Alix— "Oh! Where are you?"

"At the Traveler's Arms—that's the right name, isn't it? Or don't you even know of the existence of your village pub? I'm on my holiday—doing a bit of fishing here. Any objection to my looking you two good people up this evening after dinner?"

"No," said Alix sharply. "You mustn't come."

There was a pause, and Dick's voice, with a subtle alteration in it, spoke again.

"I beg your pardon," he said formally. "Of course I won't bother you—"

Alix broke in hastily. Of course he must think her behavior too extraordinary. It was extraordinary. Her nerves must be all to pieces. It wasn't Dick's fault that she had these dreams.

"I only meant that we were—engaged tonight," she explained, trying to make her voice sound as natural as possible. "Won't you—won't you come to dinner tomorrow night?"

But Dick evidently noticed the lack of cordiality in her tone.

"Thanks very much," he said, in the same formal voice. "But I may be moving on any time. Depends upon whether a pal of mine turns up or not. Good-by, Alix." He paused, and then added hastily, in a different tone, "Best of luck to you, my dear."

Alix hung up the receiver with a feeling of relief.

He mustn't come here, she repeated to herself. *He mustn't come here. Oh! what a fool I am! To imagine myself into a state like this. All the same, I'm glad he's not coming.*

She caught up a rustic rush hat from a table, and passed out into the garden again, pausing to look up at the name carved over the porch, *Philomel Cottage.*

"Isn't it a very fanciful name?" she had said to Gerald once before they were married. He had laughed.

"You little Cockney," he had said, affectionately. "I don't believe you have ever heard a nightingale. I'm glad you haven't. Nightingales should sing only for lovers. We'll hear them together on a summer's evening outside our own home."

And at the remembrance of how they had indeed heard them, Alix, standing in the doorway of her home, blushed happily.

It was Gerald who had found Philomel Cottage. He had come to Alix bursting with excitement. He had found the very spot for them—unique—a gem—the chance of a lifetime. And when Alix had seen it, she, too, was captivated. It was true that the situation was rather lonely—they were two miles from the nearest village—but the cottage itself was so exquisite with its Old World appearance, and its solid comfort of bathrooms, hot-water system, electric light, and telephone, that she fell a victim to its charm immediately. And then a hitch occurred. The owner, a rich man who had made it his whim, declined to rent it. He would only sell.

Gerald Martin, though possessed of a good income, was unable to touch his capital. He could raise at most a thousand pounds. The owner was asking three. But Alix, who had set her heart on the place, came to the rescue. Her own capital was easily realized, being in bearer bonds. She would contribute half of it to the purchase of the home. So Philomel Cottage became their very own, and never for a minute had Alix regretted the choice. It was true that servants did not appreciate the rural solitude—indeed at the moment they had none at all—but Alix, who had been starved of domestic life, thoroughly enjoyed cooking dainty little meals and looking after the house.

The garden which was magnificently stocked with flowers was attended to by an old man from the village who came twice a week, and Gerald Martin, who was keen on gardening, spent most of his time there.

As she rounded the corner of the house, Alix was surprised to see the old gardener in question busy over the flower beds. She was surprised because his days for work were Mondays and Fridays, and today was Wednesday.

"Why, George, what are you doing here?" she asked, as she came toward him.

The old man straightened up with a chuckle, touching the brim of an aged cap.

"I thought as how you'd be surprised, ma'am. But 'tis this way. There be a fete over to Squire's on Friday, and I sez to myself, I sez, neith Mr. Martin nor yet his good lady won't take it amiss if I comes for once on a Wednesday instead of a Friday."

"That's quite all right," said Alix. "I hope you'll enjoy yourself at the fete."

"I reckon to," said George simply. "It's a fine thing to be able to eat your fill and know all the time as it's not you as is paying for it. Squire allus has a proper sit-down tea for 'is tenants. Then I thought, too, ma'am, as I might as well see you before you goes away so as to learn your wishes for the borders. You'll have no idea when you'll be back, ma'am, I suppose?"

"But I'm not going away."

George stared at her.

"Bain't you going to Lunnon tomorrow?"

"No. What put such an idea into your head?"

George jerked his head over his shoulder.

"Met Maister down to village yesterday. He told me you was both going away to Lunnon tomorrow, and it was uncertain when you'd be back again."

"Nonsense," said Alix, laughing. "You must have misunderstood him."

All the same, she wondered exactly what it could have been that Gerald had said to lead the old man into such a curious mistake. Going to London? She never wanted to go to London again.

"I hate London," she said suddenly and harshly.

"Ah!" said George placidly. "I must have been mistook somehow, and yet he said it plain enough it seemed to me. I'm glad you're stopping on here—I don't hold with all this gallivanting about, and I don't think nothing of Lunnon. I've never needed to go there. Too many moty cars—that's the trouble nowadays. Once people have got a moty car, blessed if they can stay still anywheres. Mr. Ames, wot used to have this house—nice peaceful sort of gentleman he was until he bought one of them things. Hadn't 'ad it a month before he put up this cottage for sale. A tidy lot he'd spent on it, too, with taps in all the bedrooms, and the electric light and all. 'You'll never see your money back,' I sez to him. 'It's not everyone as'll have your fad for washing themselves in every room in the house, in a manner of speaking.' But 'George,' he sez to me, 'I'll get every penny of two thousand pounds for this house.' And sure enough, he did."

"He got three thousand," said Alix, smiling.

"Two thousand," repeated George. "The sum he was asking was talked of at the time. And a very high figure it was thought to be."

"It really was three thousand," said Alix.

"Women never understand figures," said George, un-

convinced. "You'll not tell me that Mr. Ames had the face
to stand up to you, and say three thousand brazen-like in a
loud voice."

"He didn't say it to me," said Alix. "He said it to my husband."

George stooped again to his flower bed.

"The price was two thousand," he said obstinately.

Alix did not trouble to argue with him. Moving to one of
the further beds, she began to pick an armful of flowers.
The sunshine, the scent of the flowers, the faint hum of
hurrying bees, all conspired to make the day a perfect
thing.

As she moved with her fragrant posy toward the house,
Alix noticed a small dark green object, peeping from between some leaves in one of the beds. She stooped and
picked it up, recognizing it for her husband's pocket diary.
It must have fallen from his pocket when he was weeding.

She opened it, scanning the entries with some amusement. Almost from the beginning of their married life, she
had realized that the impulsive and emotional Gerald had
the uncharacteristic virtues of neatness and method. He
was extremely fussy about meals being punctual, and always planned his day ahead with the accuracy of a time
table. This morning, for instance, he had announced that
he should start for the village after breakfast—at 10:15.
And at 10:15 to the minute he had left the house.

Looking through the diary, she was amused to notice
the entry on the date of May 14th. *Marry Alix St. Peter's
2:30.*

"The big silly," murmured Alix to herself, turning the
pages.

Suddenly she stopped.

"Wednesday, June 18th—why that's today."

In the space for that day was written in Gerald's neat
precise hand: *9 p.m.* Nothing else. What had Gerald
planned to do at 9 p.m. Alix wondered. She smiled to her-

self as she realized that had this been a story, like those she had so often read, the diary would doubtless have furnished her with some sensational revelation. It would have had in it for certain the name of another woman. She fluttered the back pages idly. There were dates, appointments, cryptic references to business deals, but only one woman's name—her own.

Yet as she slipped the book into her pocket and went on with her flowers to the house, she was aware of a vague uneasiness. Those words of Dick Windyford's recurred to her, almost as though he had been at her elbow repeating them: "The man's a perfect stranger to you. You know nothing about him."

It was true. What did she know about him? After all, Gerald was forty. In forty years there must have been women in his life.

Alix shook herself impatiently. She must not give way to these thoughts. She had a far more instant preoccupation to deal with. Should she, or should she not, tell her husband that Dick Windyford had rung her up?

There was the possibility to be considered that Gerald might have already run across him in the village. But in that case he would be sure to mention it to her immediately upon his return and matters would be taken out of her hands. Otherwise—what? Alix was aware of a distinct desire to say nothing about it. Gerald had always shown himself kindly disposed toward the other. "Poor devil," he had said once, "I believe he's just as keen on you as I am. Hard luck on him to be shelved." He had had no doubts of Alix's own feelings.

If she told him, he was sure to suggest asking Dick Windyford to Philomel Cottage. Then she would have to explain that Dick had proposed it himself, and that she had made an excuse to prevent his coming. And when he asked her why she had done so, what could she say? Tell him her dream? But he would only laugh—or, worse, see that she attached an importance to it which he did not. Then he would think—oh, he might think anything!

In the end, rather shamefacedly, Alix decided to say nothing. It was the first secret she had ever kept from her husband, and the consciousness of it made her feel ill at ease.

When she heard Gerald returning from the village shortly before lunch, she hurried into the kitchen and pretended to be busy with the cooking so as to hide her confusion.

It was evident at once that Gerald had seen nothing of Dick Windyford. Alix felt at once relieved and embarrassed. She was definitely committed now to a policy of concealment. For the rest of the day she was nervous and absent-minded, starting at every sound, but her husband seemed to notice nothing. He himself seemed to have his thoughts far away, and once or twice she had to speak a second time before he answered some trivial remark of hers.

It was not until after their simple evening meal, when they were sitting in the oak-beamed living-room with the windows thrown open to let in the sweet night air scented with the perfume of the mauve and white stocks that grew outside, that Alix remembered the pocket diary, and seized upon it gladly to distract her thoughts from their doubt and perplexity.

"Here's something you've been watering the flowers with," she said, and threw it into his lap.

"Dropped it in the border, did I?"

"Yes, I know all your secrets now."

"Not guilty," said Gerald, shaking his head.

"What about your assignation at nine o'clock tonight?"

"Oh! that—" he seemed taken back for a moment, then he smiled as though something afforded him particular amusement. "It's an assignation with a particularly nice girl, Alix. She's got brown hair and blue eyes and she's particularly like you."

"I don't understand," said Alix, with mock severity. "You're evading the point."

"No, I'm not. As a matter of fact, that's a reminder that I'm going to develop some negatives tonight, and I want you to help me."

Gerald Martin was an enthusiastic photographer. He had a somewhat old-fashioned camera, but with an excellent lens, and he developed his own plates in a small cellar which he had fitted up as a dark room. He was never tired of posing Alix in different positions.

"And it must be done at nine o'clock precisely," said Alix teasingly.

Gerald looked a little vexed.

"My dear girl," he said, with a shade of testiness in his manner, "one should always plan a thing for a definite time. Then one gets through one's work properly."

Alix sat for a minute or two in silence watching her husband as he lay in his chair smoking, his dark head flung back and the clear-cut lines of his clean-shaven face showing up against the somber background. And suddenly, from some unknown source, a wave of panic surged over her, so that she cried out before she could stop herself. "Oh! Gerald, I wish I knew more about you."

Her husband turned an astonished face upon her.

"But, my dear Alix, you do know all about me. I've told you of my boyhood in Northumberland, of my life in South Africa, and these last ten years in Canada which have brought me success."

"Oh, business!"

Gerald laughed suddenly.

"I know what you mean—love affairs. You women are all the same. Nothing interests you but the personal element."

Alix felt her throat go dry, as she muttered indistinctly, "Well, but there must have been—love affairs. I mean—

If I only knew—"

There was silence again for a minute or two. Gerald Martin was frowning, a look of indecision on his face. When he spoke, it was gravely, without a trace of his former bantering manner.

"Do you think it wise, Alix—this Bluebeard's-chamber business? There have been women in my life, yes. I don't deny it. You wouldn't believe me if I did deny it. But I can swear to you truthfully that not one of them meant anything to me."

There was a ring of sincerity in his voice which comforted the listening wife.

"Satisfied, Alix?" he asked, with a smile. Then he looked at her with a shade of curiosity.

"What has turned your mind onto these unpleasant subjects tonight of all nights? You never mentioned them before."

Alix got up and began to walk about restlessly.

"Oh! I don't know," she said. "I've been nervy all day."

"That's odd," said Gerald, in a low voice, as though speaking to himself. "That's very odd."

"Why is it odd?"

"Oh, my dear girl, don't flash out at me so. I only said it was odd because as a rule you're so sweet and serene."

Alix forced a smile.

"Everything's conspired to annoy me today," she confessed. "Even old George had got some ridiculous idea into his head that we were going away to London. He said you had told him so."

"Where did you see him?" asked Gerald sharply.

"He came to work today instead of Friday."

"The old fool," said Gerald angrily.

Alix stared in surprise. Her husband's face was convulsed with rage. She had never seen him so angry. Seeing her astonishment, Gerald made an effort to regain control of himself.

"Well, he *is* a stupid old fool," he protested.

"What can you have said to make him think that?"

"I? I never said anything. At least— Oh, yes, I remember. I made some weak joke about being 'off to London in the morning' and I suppose he took it seriously. Or else he didn't hear properly. You undeceived him, of course?"

He waited anxiously for her reply.

"Of course, but he's the sort of old man who if once he gets an idea in his head—well, it isn't so easy to get it out again."

Then she told him of the gardener's insistence on the sum asked for the cottage.

Gerald was silent for a minute or two, then he said slowly, "Ames was willing to take two thousand in cash and the remaining thousand on mortgage. That's the origin of that mistake, I fancy."

"Very likely," agreed Alix.

Then she looked up at the clock, and pointed to it with a mischievous finger.

"We ought to be getting down to it, Gerald. Five minutes behind schedule."

A very peculiar smile came over Gerald Martin's face.

"I've changed my mind," he said quietly. "I shall not do any photography tonight."

A woman's mind is a curious thing. When she went to bed that Wednesday night, Alix's mind was contented and at rest. Her momentarily assailed happiness reasserted itself, triumphant as of yore.

But by the evening of the following day, she realized that some subtle forces were at work undermining it. Dick Windyford had not rung up again, nevertheless she felt what she supposed to be his influence at work. Again and again those words of his recurred to her. "The man's a perfect stranger. You know nothing about him." And with them came the memory of her husband's face, photographed clearly on her brain as he said, "Do you think it wise, Alix, this Bluebeard's-chamber business?" Why had he said that? What had he meant by those words?

There had been warning in them—a hint of menace. It was as though he had said in effect—"You had better not pry into my life, Alix. You may get a nasty shock if you do." True, a few minutes later, he had sworn to her that there had been no woman in his life that mattered—but Alix tried in vain to recapture her sense of his sincerity. Was he not bound to swear that?

By Friday morning, Alix had convinced herself that there had been a woman in Gerald's life—a Bluebeard's chamber that he had sedulously sought to conceal from her. Her jealousy, slow to awaken, was now rampant.

Was it a woman he had been going to meet that night, at 9 p.m.? Was his story of photographs to develop a lie invented upon the spur of the moment? With a queer sense of shock Alix realized that ever since she had found that pocket diary she had been in torment. And there had been nothing in it. That was the irony of the whole thing.

Three days ago she would have sworn that she knew her husband through and through. Now it seemed to her that he was a stranger of whom she knew nothing. She remembered his unreasonable anger against old George, so at variance with his usual good-tempered manner. A small thing, perhaps, but it showed her that she did not really know the man who was her husband.

There were several little things required on Friday from the village to carry them over the week-end. In the afternoon Alix suggested that she should go for them while Gerald remained in the garden, but somewhat to her surprise he opposed this plan vehemently, and insisted on going himself while she remained at home. Alix was forced to give way to him, but his insistence surprised and alarmed her. Why was he so anxious to prevent her going to the village?

Suddenly an explanation suggested itself to her which made the whole thing clear. Was it not possible that, while saying nothing to her, Gerald had indeed come across Dick Windyford? Her own jealousy, entirely dormant at the time of their marriage, had only developed afterward. Might it not be the same with Gerald? Might he not be anxious to prevent her seeing Dick Windyford again? This explanation was so consistent with the facts, and so comforting to Alix's perturbed mind, that she embraced it eagerly.

Yet when tea time had come and past, she was restless and ill at ease. She was struggling with a temptation that had assailed her ever since Gerald's departure. Finally, pacifying her conscience with the assurance that the room did need a thorough tidying, she went upstairs to her husband's dressing-room. She took a duster with her to keep up the pretense of housewifery.

If I were only sure, she repeated to herself. *If I could only be sure.*

In vain she told herself that anything compromising would have been destroyed ages ago. Against that she argued that men do sometimes keep the most damning piece of evidence through an exaggerated sentimentality.

In the end Alix succumbed. Her cheeks burning with the shame of her action, she hunted breathlessly through packets of letters and documents, turned out the drawers, even went through the pockets of her husband's clothes. Only two drawers eluded her—the lower drawer of the chest of drawers and the small right-hand drawer of the writing desk were both locked. But Alix was by now lost to all shame. In one of those drawers she was convinced that she would find evidence of this imaginary woman of the past who obsessed her.

She remembered that Gerald had left his keys lying carelessly on the sideboard downstairs. She fetched them and tried them one by one. The third key fitted the writing table drawer. Alix pulled it open eagerly. There was a check book and a wallet well stuffed with notes, and at the back of the drawer a packet of letters tied up with a piece of tape.

Her breath coming unevenly, Alix untied the tape. Then a deep burning blush overspread her face, and she dropped the letters back into the drawer, closing and re-locking it. For the letters were her own, written to Gerald Martin before she married him.

She turned now to the chest of drawers, more with a wish to feel that she had left nothing undone, than from any expectation of finding what she sought. She was ashamed and almost convinced of the madness of her obsession.

To her annoyance none of the keys on Gerald's bunch fitted the drawer in question. Not to be defeated, Alix went into the other rooms and brought back a selection of keys with her. To her satisfaction, the key of the spare room wardrobe also fitted the chest of drawers. She unlocked the drawer and pulled it open. But there was nothing in it but a roll of newspaper clippings already dirty and discolored with age.

Alix breathed a sigh of relief. Nevertheless she glanced at the clippings, curious to know what subject had interested Gerald so much that he had taken the trouble to keep the dusty roll. They were nearly all American papers, dated some seven years ago, and dealing with the trial of the notorious swindler and bigamist, Charles LeMaitre. LeMaitre had been suspected of doing away with his women victims. A skeleton had been found beneath the floor of one of the houses he had rented, and most of the women he had "married" had never been heard of again.

He had defended himself from the charge with consummate skill, aided by some of the best legal talent in the United States. The Scottish verdict of "Non proven" might perhaps have stated the case best. In its absence, he was found Not Guilty on the capital charge, though sentenced to a long term of imprisonment on the other charges preferred against him.

Alix remembered the excitement caused by the case at the time, and also the sensation aroused by the escape of LeMaitre some three years later. He had never been recaptured. The personality of the man and his extraordinary power over women had been discussed at great length in the English papers at the time, together with an account of his excitability in court, his passionate protestations, and his occasional sudden physical collapses, due to the fact that he had a weak heart, though the ignorant accredited it to his dramatic powers.

There was a picture of him in one of the clippings Alix held, and she studied it with some interest—a long-bearded, scholarly looking gentleman. It reminded her of someone, but for the moment she could not tell who that someone was. She had never known that Gerald took an interest in crime and famous trials, though she knew that it was a hobby with many men.

Who was it the face reminded her of? Suddenly, with a shock, she realized that it was Gerald himself. The eyes and brows bore a strong resemblance to him. Perhaps he had kept the cutting for that reason. Her eyes went on to the paragraph beside the picture. Certain dates, it seemed, had been entered in the accused's pocketbook, and it was contended that these were dates when he had done away with his victims. Then a woman gave evidence and identified the prisoner positively by the fact that he had a mole on his left wrist, just below the palm of the left hand.

Alix dropped the papers from a nerveless hand, and swayed as she stood. *On his left wrist, just below the palm, Gerald had a small scar—*

The room whirled round her. Afterward it struck her as strange that she should have leaped at once to such absolute certainty. Gerald Martin was Charles LeMaitre! She knew it and accepted it in a flash. Disjointed fragments whirled through her brain, like pieces of a jigsaw puzzle fitting into place.

The money paid for the house—her money—her money only. The bearer bonds she had entrusted to his keeping. Even her dream appeared in its true significance. Deep down in her, her subconscious self had always feared Gerald Martin and wished to escape from him. And it was to Dick Windyford this self of hers had looked for help. That, too, was why she was able to accept the truth so easily, without doubt or hesitation. She was to have been another of LeMaitre's victims. Very soon, perhaps.

A half cry escaped her as she remembered something. Wednesday 9 p.m. The cellar, with the flagstones that were so easily raised. Once before, he had buried one of his victims in a cellar. It had been all planned for Wednesday night. But to write it down beforehand in that methodical manner—insanity! No, it was logical. Gerald always made a memorandum of his engagements—murder was, to him, a business proposition like any other.

But what had saved her? What could possibly have saved her? Had he relented at the last minute? No—in a flash the answer came to her. Old George. She understood now her husband's uncontrollable anger. Doubtless he had paved the way by telling everyone he met that they were going to London the next day. Then George had come to work unexpectedly, had mentioned London to her, and she had contradicted the story. Too risky to do away with her that night, with old George repeating that conversation. But what an escape! If she had not happened to mention that trivial matter—Alix shuddered.

But there was no time to be lost. She must get away at once—before he came back. For nothing on earth would she spend another night under the same roof with him. She hurriedly replaced the roll of clippings in the drawer, shut it to and locked it.

And then she stayed motionless as though frozen to

stone. She had heard the creak of the gate into the road. Her husband had returned.

For a moment Alix stayed as though petrified, then she crept on tiptoe to the window, looking out from behind the shelter of the curtain.

Yes, it was her husband. He was smiling to himself and humming a little tune. In his hand he held an object which almost made the terrified girl's heart stop beating. It was a brand new spade.

Alix leaped to a knowledge born of instinct. *It was to be tonight.*

But there was still a chance. Gerald, still humming his little tune, went round to the back of the house.

He's going to put it in the cellar—ready, thought Alix with a shiver.

Without hesitating a moment, she ran down the stairs and out of the cottage. But just as she emerged from the door, her husband came round the other side of the house.

"Hullo," he said. "Where are you running off to in such a hurry?"

Alix strove desperately to appear calm and as usual. Her chance was gone for the moment, but if she was careful not to arouse his suspicions, it would come again later. Even now, perhaps.

"I was going to walk to the end of the lane and back," she said, in a voice that sounded weak and uncertain to her own ears.

"Right," said Gerald, "I'll come with you."

"No—please, Gerald. I'm—nervy, headachy—I'd rather go alone."

He looked at her attentively. She fancied a momentary suspicion gleamed in his eye.

"What's the matter with you, Alix? You're pale—trembling."

"Nothing," she forced herself to be brusque—smiling. "I've got a headache, that's all. A walk will do me good."

"Well, it's no good you're saying you don't want me," declared Gerald with his easy laugh. "I'm coming whether you want me or not."

She dared not protest further. If he suspected that she knew—

With an effort she managed to regain something of her normal manner. Yet she had an uneasy feeling that he looked at her sideways every now and then, as though not quite satisfied. She felt that his suspicions were not completely allayed.

When they returned to the house, he insisted on her lying down, and brought some Eau de Cologne to bathe her temples. He was, as ever, the devoted husband, yet Alix felt herself as helpless as though bound hand and foot in a trap.

Not for a minute would he leave her alone. He went with her into the kitchen and helped her to bring in the simple cold dishes she had already prepared. Supper was a meal that choked her, yet she forced herself to eat, and even to appear gay and natural. She knew now that she was fighting for her life. She was alone with this man, miles from help, absolutely at his mercy. Her only chance was so to lull his suspicions that he would leave her alone for a few moments—long enough for her to get to the telephone in the hall and summon assistance. That was her only hope now. He would overtake her if she took to flight long before she could reach assistance.

A momentary hope flashed over her as she remembered how he had abandoned his plan before. Suppose she told him that Dick Windyford was coming up to see them that evening?

The words trembled on her lips—then she rejected them hastily. This man would not be balked a second time. There was a determination, an elation underneath his calm bearing that sickened her. She would only precipitate the crime. He would murder her there and then, and calmly ring up Dick Windyford with a tale of having been suddenly called away. Oh! if only Dick Windyford were coming to the house this evening. If Dick—

A sudden idea flashed into her mind. She looked sharply sideways at her husband as though she feared that he might read her mind. With the forming of a plan, her courage was reinforced. She became so completely natural in manner that she marveled at herself. She felt that Gerald now was completely reassured.

She made the coffee and took it out to the porch where they often sat on fine evenings.

"By the way," said Gerald suddenly, "we'll do those photographs later."

Alix felt a shiver run through her, but she replied nonchalantly, "Can't you manage alone? I'm rather tired tonight."

"It won't take long." He smiled to himself. "And I can promise you you won't be tired afterward."

The words seemed to amuse him. Alix shuddered. Now or never was the time to carry out her plan.

She rose to her feet.

"I'm just going to telephone to the butcher," she announced nonchalantly. "Don't you bother to move."

"To the butcher? At this time of night?"

"His shop's shut, of course, silly. But he's in his house all right. And tomorrow's Saturday, and I want him to bring me some veal cutlets early, before someone else grabs them from him. The old dear will do anything for me."

She passed quickly into the house, closing the door behind her. She heard Gerald say, "Don't shut the door," and was quick with her light reply. "It keeps the moths out. I hate moths. Are you afraid I'm going to make love to the butcher, silly?"

Once inside she snatched down the telephone receiver and gave the number of the Traveler's Arms. She was put through at once.

"Mr. Windyford? Is he still there? May I speak to him?"

Then her heart gave a sickening thump. The door was pushed open and her husband came into the hall.

"Do go away, Gerald," she said pettishly. "I hate anyone listening when I'm telephoning."

He merely laughed and threw himself into a chair.

"Sure it really is the butcher you're telephoning to?" he quizzed.

Alix was in despair. Her plan had failed. In a minute Dick Windyford would come to the phone. Should she risk all and cry out an appeal for help? Would he grasp what she meant before Gerald wrenched her away from the phone? Or would he merely treat it as a practical joke?

And then as she nervously depressed and released the little key in the receiver she was holding, which permits the voice to be heard or not heard at the other end, another plan flashed into her head.

"It will be difficult," she thought. "It means keeping my head, and thinking of the right words, and not faltering for a moment, but I believe I could do it. I *must* do it."

And at that minute she heard Dick Windyford's voice at the other end of the phone.

Alix drew a deep breath. Then she depressed the key firmly and spoke.

"Mrs. Martin speaking—from Philomel Cottage. *Please come* (she released the key) tomorrow morning with six nice veal cutlets (she depressed the key again) *It's very important* (she released the key) Thank you so much, Mr. Hexworthy, you don't mind my ringing you up so late, I hope, but those veal cutlets are really a matter of (she depressed the key again) *life or death* . . . (she released it) Very well—tomorrow morning—(she depressed it) *as soon as possible . . .*"

She replaced the receiver on the hook and turned to face her husband, breathing hard.

"So that's how you talk to your butcher, is it?" said Gerald.

"It's the feminine touch," said Alix lightly.

She was simmering with excitement. He had suspected nothing. Surely Dick, even if he didn't understand, would come.

She passed into the sitting-room and switched on the electric light. Gerald followed her.

"You seem very full of spirits now," he said, watching her curiously.

"Yes," said Alix, "my headache's gone."

She sat down in her usual seat and smiled at her husband, as he sank into his own chair opposite her. She was saved. It was only five and twenty past eight. Long before nine o'clock Dick would have arrived.

"I didn't think much of that coffee you gave me," complained Gerald. "It tasted very bitter."

"It's a new kind I was trying. We won't have it again if you don't like it, dear."

Alix took up a piece of needlework and began to stitch. She felt complete confidence in her own ability to keep up the part of the devoted wife. Gerald read a few pages of his book. Then he glanced up at the clock and tossed the book away.

"Half past eight. Time to go down to the cellar and start work."

The work slipped from Alix's fingers.

"Oh! Not yet. Let us wait until nine o'clock."

"No, my girl, half past eight. That's the time I fixed. You'll be able to get to bed all the earlier."

"But I'd rather wait until nine."

"Half past eight," said Gerald obstinately. "You know when I fix a time, I always stick to it. Come along, Alix. I'm not going to wait a minute longer."

Alix looked up at him, and in spite of herself she felt a wave of terror slide over her. The mask had been lifted;

Gerald's hands were twitching; his eyes were shining with excitement; he was continually passing his tongue over his dry lips. He no longer cared to conceal his excitement.

Alix thought, *It's true—he can't wait—he's like a madman.*

He strode over to her, and jerked her onto her feet with a hand on her shoulder.

"Come on, my girl—or I'll carry you there."

His tone was gay, but there was an undisguised ferocity behind it that appalled her. With a supreme effort she jerked herself free and clung cowering against the wall. She was powerless. She couldn't get away—she couldn't do anything—and he was coming toward her.

"Now, Alix—"

"No—no."

She screamed, her hands held out impotently to ward him off.

"Gerald—stop—I've got something to tell you, something to confess—"

He did stop.

"To confess?" he said curiously.

"Yes, to confess." She went on desperately, seeking to hold his arrested attention. "Something I ought to have told you before."

A look of contempt swept over his face. The spell was broken.

"A former lover, I suppose," he sneered.

"No," said Alix. "Something else. You'd call it, I expect—yes, you'd call it a crime."

And at once she saw that she had struck the right note. Again his attention was arrested, held. Seeing that, her nerve came back to her. She felt mistress of the situation once more.

"You had better sit down again," she said quietly.

She herself crossed the room to her old chair and sat down. She even stooped and picked up her needlework.

But behind her calmness she was thinking and inventing feverishly. For the story she invented must hold his interest until help arrived.

"I told you," she said, "that I had been a shorthand typist for fifteen years. That was not entirely true. There were two intervals. The first occurred when I was twenty-two. I came across a man, an elderly man with a little property. He fell in love with me and asked me to marry him. I accepted. We were married." She paused. "I induced him to insure his life in my favor."

She saw a sudden keen interest spring up in her husband's face, and went on with renewed assurance.

"During the war I worked for a time in a Hospital Dispensary. There I had the handling of all kinds of rare drugs and poisons. Yes, poisons."

She paused reflectively. He was keenly interested now, not a doubt of it. The murderer is bound to have an interest in murder. She had gambled on that, and succeeded. She stole a glance at the clock. It was five and twenty to nine.

"There is one poison—it is a little white powder. A pinch of it means death. You know something about poisons perhaps?"

She put the question in some trepidation. If he did, she would have to be careful.

"No," said Gerald, "I know very little about them."

She drew a breath of relief. This made her task easier.

"You have heard of Hyoscine, of course? This is a drug that acts much the same way, but it is absolutely untraceable. Any doctor would give a certificate of heart failure. I stole a small quantity of this drug and kept it by me."

She paused, marshaling her forces.

"Go on," said Gerald.

"No. I'm afraid. I can't tell you. Another time."

"Now," he said impatiently. "I want to hear."

"We had been married a month. I was very good to my

elderly husband, very kind and devoted. He spoke in praise of me to all the neighbors. Everyone knew what a devoted wife I was. I always made his coffee myself every evening. One evening, when we were alone together, I put a pinch of the deadly alkaloid in his cup."

Alix paused, and carefully rethreaded her needle. She, who had never acted in her life, rivaled the greatest actress in the world at this moment. She was actually living the part of the cold-blooded poisoner.

"It was very peaceful. I sat watching him. Once he gasped a little and asked for air. I opened the window. Then he said he could not move from his chair. Presently he died."

She stopped, smiling. It was a quarter to nine. Surely they would come soon.

"How much," said Gerald, "was the insurance money?"

"About two thousand pounds. I speculated with it, and lost it. I went back to my office work. But I never meant to remain there long. Then I met another man. I had stuck to my maiden name at the office. He didn't know I had been married before. He was a younger man, rather good-looking, and quite well off. We were married quietly in Sussex. He didn't want to insure his life, but of course he made a will in my favor. He liked me to make his coffee myself, also, just as my first husband had done." Alix smiled reflectively, and added simply, "I make very good coffee."

Then she went on.

"I had several friends in the village where we were living. They were very sorry for me, with my husband dying suddenly of heart failure one evening after dinner. I didn't quite like the doctor. I don't think he suspected me, but he was certainly very surprised at my husband's sudden death. I don't quite know why I drifted back to the office again. Habit, I suppose. My second husband left about four thousand pounds. I didn't speculate with it this time. I invested it. Then, you see—"

But she was interrupted. Gerald Martin, his face suffused with blood, half choking, was pointing a shaking forefinger at her.

"The coffee—my God! The coffee!"

She stared at him.

"I understand now why it was bitter. You devil. You've poisoned me."

His hands gripped the arms of his chair. He was ready to spring upon her.

"You've poisoned me."

Alix had retreated from him to the fireplace. Now, terrified, she opened her lips to deny—and then paused. In another minute he would spring upon her. She summoned all her strength. Her eyes held his steadily, compellingly.

"Yes," she said, "I poisoned you. Already the poison is working. At this minute you can't move from your chair—you can't move—"

If she could keep him there—even a few minutes—

Ah! what was that? Footsteps on the road. The creak of the gate. Then footsteps on the path outside. The door of the hall opened—

"You can't move," she said again.

Then she slipped past him and fled headlong from the room to fall, half fainting, into Dick Windyford's arms.

"My God! Alix!" he cried.

Then he turned to the man with him, a tall, stalwart figure in policeman's uniform.

"Go and see what's been happening in that room."

He laid Alix carefully down on a couch and bent over her.

"My little girl," he murmured. "My poor little girl. What have they been doing to you?"

Her eyelids fluttered and her lips just murmured his name.

Dick was aroused from tumultuous thoughts by the

policeman's touching him on the arm.

"There's nothing in that room, sir, but a man sitting in a chair. Looks as though he'd had some kind of bad fright, and—"

"Yes?"

"Well, sir, he's—dead."

They were startled by hearing Alix's voice. She spoke as though in some kind of dream.

"And presently," she said, almost as though she were quoting from something, "he died."

ACCIDENT

"And I tell you this—it's the same woman—not a doubt of it!" Captain Haydock looked into the eager, vehement face of his friend and sighed. He wished Evans would not be so positive and so jubilant. In the course of a career spent at sea, the old sea captain had learned to leave things that did not concern him well alone. His friend Evans, late C.I.D. Inspector, had a different philosophy of life. "Acting on information received—" had been his motto in early days, and he had improved upon it to the extent of finding out his own information. Inspector Evans had been a very smart, wide-awake officer, and had justly earned the promotion which had been his. Even now, when he had retired from the force, and had settled down in the country cottage of his dreams, his professional instinct was still active.

"Don't often forget a face," he reiterated complacently. "Mrs. Anthony—yes, it's Mrs. Anthony right enough. When you said Mrs. Merrowdene—I knew her at once."

Captain Haydock stirred uneasily. The Merrowdenes were his nearest neighbors, barring Evans himself, and this identifying of Mrs. Merrowdene with a former heroine of a *cause célèbre* distressed him.

"It's a long time ago," he said rather weakly.

"Nine years," said Evans, accurate as ever. "Nine years and three months. You remember the case?"

"In a vague sort of way."

"Anthony turned out to be an arsenic eater," said Evans, "so they acquitted her."

"Well, why shouldn't they?"

"No reason in the world. Only verdict they could give on the evidence. Absolutely correct."

"Then, that's all right," said Haydock. "And I don't see what we're bothering about."

"Who's bothering?"

"I thought you were."

"Not at all."

"The thing's over and done with," summed up the Captain. "If Mrs. Merrowdene at one time of her life was unfortunate enough to be tried and acquitted of murder—"

"It's not usually considered unfortunate to be acquitted," put in Evans.

"You know what I mean," said Captain Haydock, irritably. "If the poor lady has been through that harrowing experience, it's no business of ours to rake it up, is it?"

Evans did not answer.

"Come now, Evans. The lady was innocent—you've just said so."

"I didn't say she was innocent. I said she was acquitted."

"It's the same thing."

"Not always."

Captain Haydock, who had commenced to tap his pipe out against the side of his chair, stopped and sat up with a very alert expression.

"Hullo-ullo-ullo," he said. "The wind's in that quarter, is it? You think she wasn't innocent?"

"I wouldn't say that. I just—don't know. Anthony was in the habit of taking arsenic. His wife got it for him. One day, by mistake, he takes far too much. Was the mistake his or his wife's? Nobody could tell, and the jury very properly gave her the benefit of the doubt. That's all quite right and I'm not finding fault with it. All the same—I'd like to know."

Captain Haydock transferred his attention to his pipe once more.

"Well," he said comfortably, "it's none of our business."

"I'm not so sure."

"But, surely—"

"Listen to me a minute. This man, Merrowdene—in his laboratory last evening, fiddling round with tests—you remember—"

"Yes. He mentioned Marsh's test for arsenic. Said you would know all about it—it was in your line—and chuckled. He wouldn't have said that if he'd thought for one moment—"

Evans interrupted him.

"You mean he wouldn't have said that if he knew. They've been married how long—six years, you told me? I bet you anything he has no idea his wife is the once notorious Mrs. Anthony."

"And he will certainly not know it from me," said Captain Haydock stiffly.

Evans paid no attention, but went on.

"You interrupted me just now. After Marsh's test, Merrowdene heated a substance in a test tube, the metallic residue he dissolved in water and then precipitated it by adding silver nitrate. That was a test for chlorates. A neat, unassuming little test. But I chanced to read these words in a book that stood open on the table. 'H_2SO_4 decomposes chlorates with evolution of CL_{2O_4}. If heated, violent explosions occur, the mixture ought therefore to be kept cool and only very small quantities used.'"

Haydock stared at his friend.

"Well, what about it?"

"Just this. In my profession we've got tests, too—tests for murder. There's adding up the facts—weighing them, dissecting the residue when you've allowed for prejudice and the general inaccuracy of witnesses. But there's another test for murder—one that is fairly accurate, but rather—dangerous! A murderer is seldom content with one crime. Give him time and a lack of suspicion and he'll commit another. You catch a man—has he murdered his wife or hasn't he?—perhaps the case isn't very black against him. Look into his past—if you find that he's had several wives—and that they've all died, shall we say—rather curiously?—then you know! I'm not speaking legally, you understand. I'm speaking of moral certainty. Once you know, you can go ahead looking for evidence."

"Well?"

"I'm coming to the point. That's all right if there is a past to look into. But suppose you catch your murderer at his or her first crime? Then that test will be one from which you get no reaction. But the prisoner acquitted—starting life under another name. Will or will not the murderer repeat the crime?"

"That's a horrible idea."

"Do you still say it's none of our business?"

"Yes, I do. You've no reason to think that Mrs. Merrowdene is anything but a perfectly innocent woman."

The ex-Inspector was silent for a moment. Then he said slowly, "I told you that we looked into her past and found nothing. That's not quite true. There was a stepfather. As a girl of eighteen she had a fancy for some young man—and her stepfather exerted his authority to keep them apart. She and her stepfather went for a walk along a rather dangerous part of the cliff. There was an accident—the stepfather went too near the edge—it gave way and he went over and was killed."

"You don't think—"

"It was an accident. Accident! Anthony's overdose of arsenic was an accident. She'd never have been tried if it hadn't transpired that there was another man—he sheered off, by the way. Looked as though he weren't satisfied even if the jury were. I tell you, Haydock, where that woman is concerned I'm afraid of another—accident!"

The old Captain shrugged his shoulders.

"Well, I don't know how you're going to guard against that."

"Neither do I," said Evans ruefully.

"I should leave well enough alone," said Captain Haydock. "No good ever came of butting into other people's affairs."

But that advice was not palatable to the ex-Inspector. He was a man of patience but determination. Taking leave of his friend, he sauntered down to the village, revolving in his mind the possibilities of some kind of successful action.

Turning into the post office to buy some stamps, he ran into the object of his solicitude, George Merrowdene. The ex-chemistry professor was a small, dreamy-looking man, gentle and kindly in manner, and usually completely absent-minded. He recognized the other and greeted him amicably, stooping to recover the letters that the impact had caused him to drop on the ground. Evans stooped also and, more rapid in his movements than the other, secured them first, handing them back to their owner with an apology.

He glanced down at them in doing so, and the address on the topmost suddenly awakened all his suspicions anew. It bore the name of a well-known insurance firm.

Instantly his mind was made up. The guileless George Merrowdene hardly realized how it came about that he and the ex-Inspector were strolling down the village together, and still less could he have said how it came about that the conversation should come round to the subject of life insurance.

Evans had no difficulty in attaining his object. Merrowdene of his own accord volunteered the information that he had just insured his life for his wife's benefit, and asked Evans's opinion of the company in question.

"I made some rather unwise investments," he explained. "As a result, my income has diminished. If anything were to happen to me, my wife would be left very badly off. This insurance will put things right."

"She didn't object to the idea?" inquired Evans casually. "Some ladies do, you know. Feel it's unlucky—that sort of thing."

"Oh, Margaret is very practical," said Merrowdene, smiling. "Not at all superstitious. In fact, I believe it was her idea originally. She didn't like my being so worried."

Evans had got the information he wanted. He left the other shortly afterward, and his lips were set in a grim line. The late Mr. Anthony had insured his life in his wife's favor a few weeks before his death.

Accustomed to rely on his instincts, he was perfectly sure in his own mind. But how to act was another matter. He wanted, not to arrest a criminal red-handed, but to prevent a crime being committed and that was a very different and a very much more difficult thing.

All day he was very thoughtful. There was a Primrose League Fete that afternoon held in the grounds of the local squire, and he went to it, indulging in the penny dip, guessing the weight of a pig, and shying at coconuts, all with the same look of abstracted concentration on his face. He even indulged in half a crown's worth of Zara the Crystal Gazer, smiling a little to himself as he did so, remembering his own activities against fortunetellers in his official days.

He did not pay very much heed to her singsong, droning voice till the end of a sentence held his attention.

"—and you will very shortly—very shortly indeed—be engaged on a matter of life or death—life or death to one person."

"Eh—what's that?" he asked abruptly.

"A decision—you have a decision to make. You must be very careful—very, very careful. If you were to make a mistake—the smallest mistake—"

"Yes?"

The fortuneteller shivered. Inspector Evans knew it was all nonsense, but he was nevertheless impressed.

"I warn you—you must not make a mistake. If you do, I see the result clearly, a death."

Odd, damned odd! A death. Fancy her lighting upon that!

"If I make a mistake a death will result? Is that it?"

"Yes."

"In that case," said Evans, rising to his feet and handing over half a crown, "I mustn't make a mistake, eh?"

He spoke lightly enough, but as he went out of the tent, his jaw set determinedly. Easy to say—not so easy to be sure of doing. He mustn't make a slip. A life, a valuable human life depended on it.

And there was no one to help him. He looked across at the figure of his friend Haydock in the distance. No help there. "Leave things alone," was Haydock's motto. And that wouldn't do here.

Haydock was talking to a woman. She moved away from him and came toward Evans, and the Inspector recognized her. It was Mrs. Merrowdene. On an impulse he put himself deliberately in her path.

Mrs. Merrowdene was rather a fine-looking woman. She had a broad, serene brow, very beautiful brown eyes, and a placid expression. She had the look of an Italian Madonna which she heightened by parting her hair in the middle and looping it over her ears. She had a deep, rather sleepy voice.

She smiled up at Evans, a contented, welcoming smile.

"I thought it was you, Mrs. Anthony—I mean Mrs. Merrowdene," he said glibly.

He made the slip deliberately, watching her without seeming to do so. He saw her eyes widen, heard the quick intake of her breath. But her eyes did not falter. She gazed at him steadily and proudly.

"I was looking for my husband," she said quietly. "Have you seen him anywhere about?"

"He was over in that direction when I last saw him."

They went side by side in the direction indicated, chatting quietly and pleasantly. The Inspector felt his admiration mounting. What a woman! What self-command! What wonderful poise! A remarkable woman—and a very dangerous one. He felt sure—a very dangerous one.

He still felt very uneasy, though he was satisfied with his initial step. He had let her know that he recognized her. That would put her on her guard. She would not dare attempt anything rash. There was the question of Merrowdene. If he could be warned—

They found the little man absently contemplating a china doll which had fallen to his share in the penny dip. His wife suggested home, and he agreed eagerly. Mrs. Merrowdene turned to the Inspector.

"Won't you come back with us and have a quiet cup of tea, Mr. Evans?"

Was there a faint note of challenge in her voice? He thought there was.

"Thank you, Mrs. Merrowdene. I should like to very much."

They walked there, talking together of pleasant ordinary things. The sun shone, a breeze blew gently, everything around them was pleasant and ordinary.

Their maid was out at the Fete, Mrs. Merrowdene explained, when they arrived at the charming Old World cottage. She went into her room to remove her hat, returning to set out tea and boil the kettle on a little silver lamp. From a shelf near the fireplace she took three small bowls and saucers.

"We have some very special Chinese tea," she explained. "And we always drink it in the Chinese manner—out of bowls, not cups."

She broke off, peered into a cup and exchanged it for another, with an exclamation of annoyance.

"George—it's too bad of you. You've been taking these bowls again."

"I'm sorry, dear," said the professor apologetically. "They're such a convenient size. The ones I ordered haven't come."

"One of these days you'll poison us all," said his wife with a half laugh. "Mary finds them in the laboratory and brings them back here and never troubles to wash them out unless they've something very noticeable in them. Why, you were using one of them for potassium cyanide the other day. Really, George, it's frightfully dangerous."

Merrowdene looked a little irritated.

"Mary's no business to remove things from the laboratory. She's not to touch anything there."

"But we often leave our teacups there after tea. How is she to know? Be reasonable, dear."

The professor went into his laboratory, murmuring to himself, and with a smile Mrs. Merrowdene poured boiling water on the tea and blew out the flame of the little silver lamp.

Evans was puzzled. Yet a glimmering of light penetrated to him. For some reason or other, Mrs. Merrowdene was showing her hand. Was this to be the "accident"? Was she speaking of all this so as deliberately to prepare her alibi beforehand. So that when, one day, the "accident" happened, he would be forced to give evidence in her favor. Stupid of her, if so, because before that—

Suddenly he drew in his breath. She had poured the tea into the three bowls. One she set before him, one before herself, the other she placed on a little table by the fire near the chair her husband usually sat in, and it was as she placed this last one on the table that a little strange smile curved round her lips. It was the smile that did it.

He knew!

A remarkable woman—a dangerous woman. No waiting —no preparation. This afternoon—this very afternoon— with him here as witness. The boldness of it took his breath away.

It was clever—it was damnably clever. He would be able to prove nothing. She counted on his not suspecting—

simply because it was "so soon." A woman of lightning rapidity of thought and action.

He drew a deep breath and leaned forward.

"Mrs. Merrowdene, I'm a man of queer whims. Will you be very kind and indulge me in one of them?"

She looked inquiring but unsuspicious.

He rose, took the bowl from in front of her and crossed to the little table where he substituted it for the other. This other he brought back and placed in front of her.

"I want to see you drink this."

Her eyes met his. They were steady, unfathomable. The color slowly drained from her face.

She stretched out her hand, raised the cup. He held his breath.

Supposing all along he had made a mistake.

She raised it to her lips—at the last moment, with a shudder she leaned forward and quickly poured it into a pot containing a fern. Then she sat back and gazed at him defiantly.

He drew a long sigh of relief, and sat down again.

"Well?" she said.

Her voice had altered. It was slightly mocking—defiant.

He answered her soberly and quietly.

"You are a very clever woman, Mrs. Merrowdene. I think you understand me. There must be no—repetition. You know what I mean?"

"I know what you mean."

Her voice was even, devoid of expression. He nodded his head, satisfied. She was a clever woman, and she didn't want to be hanged.

"To your long life and to that of your husband," he said significantly and raised his tea to his lips.

Then his face changed. It contorted horribly—he tried to rise—to cry out— His body stiffened—his face went purple. He fell back sprawling over the chair—his limbs convulsed.

Mrs. Merrowdene leaned forward, watching him. A little smile crossed her lips. She spoke to him—very softly and gently.

"You made a mistake, Mr. Evans. You thought I wanted to kill George. How stupid of you—how very stupid."

She sat there a minute longer looking at the dead man, the third man who had threatened to cross her path and separate her from the man she loved.

Her smile broadened. She looked more than ever like a Madonna. Then she raised her voice and called.

"George—George. Oh! Do come here. I'm afraid there's been the most dreadful accident. Poor Mr. Evans. . . ."

THE SECOND GONG

JOAN ASHBY CAME out of her bedroom and stood a moment on the landing outside her door. She was half turning as if to go back into the room when, below her feet as it seemed, a gong boomed out.

Immediately Joan started forward almost at a run. So great was her hurry that at the top of the big staircase she collided with a young man arriving from the opposite direction.

"Hullo, Joan! Why the wild hurry?"

"Sorry, Harry. I didn't see you."

"So I gathered," said Harry Dalehouse dryly. "But as I say, why the wild haste?"

"It was the gong."

"I know. But it's only the first gong."

"No, it's the second."

"First."

"Second."

Thus arguing they had been descending the stairs. They were now in the hall, where the butler, having replaced the gongstick, was advancing toward them at a grave and dignified pace.

"It is the second," persisted Joan. "I know it is. Well, for one thing, look at the time."

Harry Dalehouse glanced up at the grandfather clock.

"Just twelve minutes past eight," he remarked. "Joan, I believe you're right, but I never heard the first one. Digby," he addressed the butler, "is this the first gong or the second?"

"The first, sir."

"At twelve minutes past eight? Digby, somebody will get the sack for this."

A faint smile showed for a minute on the butler's face.

"Dinner is being served ten minutes later tonight, sir. The master's orders."

"Incredible!" cried Harry Dalehouse. "Tut, tut! Upon my word, things are coming to a pretty pass! Wonders will never cease. What ails my revered uncle?"

"The seven-o'clock train, sir, was half an hour late, and as—" The butler broke off, as a sound like the crack of a whip was heard.

"What on earth—" said Harry. "Why, that sounded exactly like a shot."

A dark, handsome man of thirty-five came out of the drawing-room on their left.

"What was that?" he asked. "It sounded exactly like a shot."

"It must have been a car backfiring, sir," said the butler. "The road runs quite close to the house this side and the upstairs windows are open."

"Perhaps," said Joan doubtfully. "But that would be over there." She waved a hand to the right. "And I thought the noise came from here." She pointed to the left.

The dark man shook his head.

"I don't think so. I was in the drawing-room. I came out here because I thought the noise came from this direction." He nodded his head in front of him in the direction of the gong and the front door.

"East, west, and south, eh?" said the irrepressible Harry. "Well, I'll make it complete, Keene. North for me. I thought it came from behind us. Any solutions offered?"

"Well, there's always murder," said Geoffrey Keene, smiling. "I beg your pardon, Miss Ashby."

"Only a shiver," said Joan. "It's nothing. A what-do-you-call-it walking over my grave."

"A good thought—murder," said Harry. "But, alas! No groans, no blood. I fear the solution is a poacher after a rabbit."

"Seems tame, but I suppose that's it," agreed the other. "But it sounded so near. However, let's come into the drawing-room."

"Thank goodness, we're not late," said Joan fervently. "I was simply hareing it down the stairs thinking that was the second gong."

All laughing, they went into the big drawing-room.

Lytcham Close was one of the most famous old houses in England. Its owner, Hubert Lytcham Roche, was the last of a long line, and his more distant relatives were apt to remark that "Old Hubert, you know, really ought to be certified. Mad as a hatter, poor old bird."

Allowing for the exaggeration natural to friends and relatives, some truth remained. Hubert Lytcham Roche was certainly eccentric. Though a very fine musician, he was a man of ungovernable temper and had an almost abnormal sense of his own importance. People staying in the house had to respect his prejudices or else they were never asked again.

One such prejudice was his music. If he played to his guests, as he often did in the evening, absolute silence must obtain. A whispered comment, a rustle of a dress, a movement even—and he would turn round scowling fiercely, and good-by to the unlucky guest's chances of being asked again.

Another point was absolute punctuality for the crowning meal of the day. Breakfast was immaterial—you might come down at noon if you wished. Lunch also—a simple meal of cold meats and stewed fruit. But dinner was a rite, a festival, prepared by a *cordon bleu* whom he had tempted from a big hotel by the payment of a fabulous salary.

A first gong was sounded at five minutes past eight. At a quarter past eight a second gong was heard, and immediately after the door was flung open, dinner announced to the assembled guests, and a solemn procession wended

its way to the dining-room. Anyone who had the temerity
to be late for the second gong was henceforth excommunicated—and Lytcham Close shut to the unlucky diner forever.

Hence the anxiety of Joan Ashby, and also the astonishment of Harry Dalehouse, at hearing that the sacred function was to be delayed ten minutes on this particular evening. Though not very intimate with his uncle, he had
been to Lytcham Close often enough to know what a very
unusual occurrence that was.

Geoffrey Keene, who was Lytcham Roche's secretary,
was also very much surprised.

"Extraordinary," he commented. "I've never known
such a thing to happen. Are you sure?"

"Digby said so."

"He said something about a train," said Joan Ashby.
"At least I think so."

"Queer," said Keene thoughtfully. "We shall hear all
about it in due course, I suppose. But it's very odd."

Both men were silent for a moment or two, watching the
girl. Joan Ashby was a charming creature, blue-eyed and
golden-haired, with an impish glance. This was her first
visit to Lytcham Close and her invitation was at Harry's
prompting.

The door opened and Diana Cleves, the Lytcham
Roches' adopted daughter, came into the room.

There was a daredevil grace about Diana, a witchery in
her dark eyes and her mocking tongue. Nearly all men fell
for Diana and she enjoyed her conquests. A strange creature, with her alluring suggestion of warmth and her complete coldness.

"Beaten the Old Man for once," she remarked. "First
time for weeks he hasn't been here first, looking at his
watch and tramping up and down like a tiger at feeding
time."

The young men had sprung forward. She smiled entrancingly at them both—then turned to Harry. Geoffrey Keene's dark cheek flushed as he dropped back.

He recovered himself, however, a moment later as Mrs. Lytcham Roche came in. She was a tall, dark woman, naturally vague in manner, wearing floating draperies of an indeterminate shade of green. With her was a middle-aged man with a beaklike nose and a determined chin—Gregory Barling. He was a somewhat prominent figure in the financial world and, well bred on his mother's side, he had for some years been an intimate friend of Hubert Lytcham Roche.

Boom!

The gong resounded imposingly. As it died away, the door was flung open and Digby announced:

"Dinner is served."

Then, well-trained servant though he was, a look of complete astonishment flashed over his impassive face. For the first time in his memory, his master was not in the room!

That his astonishment was shared by everybody was evident. Mrs. Lytcham Roche gave a little uncertain laugh.

"Most amazing. Really—I don't know what to do."

Everybody was taken aback. The whole tradition of Lytcham Close was undermined. What could have happened? Conversation ceased. There was a strained sense of waiting.

At last the door opened once more; a sigh of relief went round only tempered by a slight anxiety as to how to treat the situation. Nothing must be said to emphasize the fact that the host had himself transgressed the stringent rule of the house.

But the newcomer was not Lytcham Roche. Instead of the big, bearded, vikinglike figure, there advanced into the long drawing-room a very small man, palpably a foreigner, with an egg-shaped head, a flamboyant mustache, and most irreproachable evening clothes.

His eyes twinkling, the newcomer advanced toward Mrs. Lytcham Roche.

"My apologies, madame," he said. "I am, I fear, a few minutes late."

"Oh, not at all!" murmured Mrs. Lytcham Roche vaguely. "Not at all, Mr.—" She paused.

"Poirot, madame. Hercule Poirot."

He heard behind him a very soft "Oh"—a gasp rather than an articulate word—a woman's ejaculation. Perhaps he was flattered.

"You knew I was coming?" he murmured gently. "*N'est-ce pas, madame?* Your husband told you."

"Oh—oh, yes," said Mrs. Lytcham Roche, her manner unconvincing in the extreme. "I mean, I suppose so. I am so terribly unpractical, M. Poirot. I never remember anything. But fortunately Digby sees to everything."

"My train, I fear, was late," said M. Poirot. "An accident on the line in front of us."

"Oh," cried Joan, "so that's why dinner was put off."

His eye came quickly round to her—a most uncannily discerning eye.

"That is something out of the usual—eh?"

"I really can't think—" began Mrs. Lytcham Roche, and then stopped. "I mean," she went on confusedly, "it's so odd. Hubert never—"

Poirot's eyes swept rapidly round the group.

"M. Lytcham Roche is not down yet?"

"No, and it's so extraordinary—" She looked appealingly at Geoffrey Keene.

"Mr. Lytcham Roche is the soul of punctuality," explained Keene. "He has not been late for dinner for—well, I don't know that he was ever late before."

To a stranger the situation must have been ludicrous—the perturbed faces and the general consternation.

"I know," said Mrs. Lytcham Roche with the air of one solving a problem. "I shall ring for Digby."

She suited the action to the word.

The butler came promptly.

"Digby," said Mrs. Lytcham Roche, "your master. Is he—"

As was customary with her, she did not finish her sentence. It was clear that the butler did not expect her to do so. He replied promptly and with understanding.

"Mr. Lytcham Roche came down at five minutes to eight and went into the study, madam."

"Oh!" She paused. "You don't think—I mean—he heard the gong?"

"I think he must have—the gong is immediately outside the study door."

"Yes, of course, of course," said Mrs. Lytcham Roche more vaguely than ever.

"Shall I inform him, madam, that dinner is ready?"

"Oh, thank you, Digby. Yes, I think—yes, yes, I should."

"I don't know," said Mrs. Lytcham Roche to her guests as the butler withdrew, "what I would do without Digby!"

A pause followed.

Then Digby re-entered the room. His breath was coming a little faster than is considered good form in a butler.

"Excuse me, madam—the study door is locked."

It was then that M. Hercule Poirot took command of the situation.

"I think," he said, "that we had better go to the study."

He led the way and everyone followed. His assumption of authority seemed perfectly natural. He was no longer a rather comic-looking guest. He was a personality and master of the situation.

He led the way out into the hall, past the staircase, past the great clock, past the recess in which stood the gong. Exactly opposite that recess was a closed door.

He tapped on it, first gently, then with increasing violence. But there was no reply. Very nimbly he dropped to his knees and applied his eye to the keyhole. He rose and looked round.

"Messieurs," he said, "we must break open this door. Immediately!"

As before no one questioned his authority. Geoffrey Keene and Gregory Barling were the two biggest men. They attacked the door under Poirot's directions. It was no easy matter. The doors of Lytcham Close were solid affairs—no modern jerry-building here. It resisted the attack valiantly, but at last it gave before the united attack of the men and crashed inward.

The house party hesitated in the doorway. They saw what they had subconsciously feared to see. Facing them was the window. On the left, between the door and the window, was a big writing table. Sitting, not at the table, but sideways to it, was a man—a big man—slouched forward in the chair. His back was to them and his face to the window, but his position told the tale. His right hand hung limply down and below it, on the carpet, was a small shining pistol.

Poirot spoke sharply to Gregory Barling.

"Take Mrs. Lytcham Roche away—and the other two ladies."

The other nodded comprehendingly. He laid a hand on his hostess's arm. She shivered.

"He has shot himself," she murmured. "Horrible!" With another shiver she permitted him to lead her away. The two girls followed.

Poirot came forward into the room, the two young men behind him.

He knelt down by the body, motioning them to keep back a little.

He found the bullet hole on the right side of the head. It had passed out the other side and had evidently struck a mirror hanging on the left-hand wall, since this was shivered. On the writing table was a sheet of paper, blank save for the word *Sorry* scrawled across it in hesitating, shaky writing.

Poirot's eyes darted back to the door.

"The key is not in the lock," he said. "I wonder—"

His hand slid into the dead man's pocket.

"Here it is," he said. "At least I think so. Have the goodness to try it, monsieur?"

Geoffrey Keene took it from him and tried it in the lock.

"That's it, all right."

"And the window?"

Harry Dalehouse strode across to it.

"Shut."

"You permit?" Very swiftly, Poirot scrambled to his feet and joined the other at the window. It was a long French window. Poirot opened it, stood a minute scrutinizing the grass just in front of it, then closed it again.

"My friends," he said, "we must telephone for the police. Until they have come and satisfied themselves that it is truly suicide nothing must be touched. Death can only have occurred about a quarter of an hour ago."

"I know," said Harry hoarsely. "We heard the shot."

"*Comment?* What is that you say?"

Harry explained with the help of Geoffrey Keene. As he finished speaking, Barling reappeared.

Poirot repeated what he had said before, and while Keene went off to telephone, Poirot requested Barling to give him a few minutes' interview.

They went into a small morning room, leaving Digby on guard outside the study door, while Harry went off to find the ladies.

"You were, I understand, an intimate friend of M. Lytcham Roche," began Poirot. "It is for that reason that I address myself to you primarily. In etiquette, perhaps, I should have spoken first to madame, but at the moment I do not think that is *pratique*."

He paused.

"I am, see you, in a delicate situation. I will lay the facts plainly before you. I am, by profession, a private detective."

The financier smiled a little.

"It is not necessary to tell me that, M. Poirot. Your name is, by now, a household word."

"Monsieur is too amiable," said Poirot, bowing. "Let us, then, proceed. I receive, at my London address, a letter from this M. Lytcham Roche. In it he says that he has reason to believe that he is being swindled of large sums of money. For family reasons, so he puts it, he does not wish to call in the police, but he desires that I should come down and look into the matter for him. Well, I agree. I come. Not quite so soon as M. Lytcham Roche wishes—for after all I have other affairs, and M. Lytcham Roche, he is not quite the King of England, though he seems to think he is."

Barling gave a wry smile.

"He did think of himself that way."

"Exactly. Oh, you comprehend—his letter showed plainly enough that he was what one calls an eccentric. He was not insane, but he was unbalanced, *n'est-ce pas?*"

"What he's just done ought to show that."

"Oh, monsieur, but suicide is not always the act of the unbalanced. The coroner's jury, they say so, but that is to spare the feelings of those left behind."

"Hubert was not a normal individual," said Barling decisively. "He was given to ungovernable rages, was a monomaniac on the subject of family pride, and had a bee in his bonnet in more ways than one. But for all that he was a shrewd man."

"Precisely. He was sufficiently shrewd to discover that he was being robbed."

"Does a man commit suicide because he's being robbed?" Barling asked.

"As you say, monsieur. Ridiculous. And that brings me

to the need for haste in the matter. For family reasons—that was the phrase he used in his letter. *Eh bien,* monsieur, you are a man of the world, you know that it is for precisely that—family reasons—that a man does commit suicide."

"You mean?"

"That it looks—on the face of it—as if *ce pauvre* monsieur had found out something further—and was unable to face what he had found out. But you perceive, I have a duty. I am already employed—commissioned—I have accepted the task. This 'family reason,' the dead man did not want it to get to the police. So I must act quickly. I must learn the truth."

"And when you have learned it?"

"Then—I must use my discretion. I must do what I can."

"I see," said Barling. He smoked for a minute or two in silence, then he said, "All the same I'm afraid I can't help you. Hubert never confided anything to me. I know nothing."

"But tell me, monsieur, who, should you say, had a chance of robbing this poor gentleman?"

"Difficult to say. Of course, there's the agent for the estate. He's a new man."

"The agent?"

"Yes. Marshall. Captain Marshall. Very nice fellow, lost an arm in the war. He came here a year ago. But Hubert liked him, I know, and trusted him, too."

"If it were Captain Marshall who was playing him false, there would be no family reasons for silence."

"N-No."

The hesitation did not escape Poirot.

"Speak, monsieur. Speak plainly, I beg of you."

"It may be gossip."

"I implore you, speak."

"Very well, then, I will. Did you notice a very attractive looking young woman in the drawing-room?"

"I noticed two very attractive looking young women."

"Oh, yes, Miss Ashby. Pretty little thing. Her first visit. Harry Dalehouse got Mrs. Lytcham Roche to ask her. No, I mean a dark girl—Diana Cleves."

"I noticed her," said Poirot. "She is one that all men would notice, I think."

"She's a little devil," burst out Barling. "She's played fast and loose with every man for twenty miles round. Someone will murder her one of these days."

He wiped his brow with a handkerchief, oblivious of the keen interest with which the other was regarding him.

"And this young lady is—"

"She's Lytcham Roche's adopted daughter. A great disappointment when he and his wife had no children. They adopted Diana Cleves—she was some kind of cousin. Hubert was devoted to her, simply worshiped her."

"Doubtless he would dislike the idea of her marrying?" suggested Poirot.

"Not if she married the right person."

"And the right person was—you, monsieur?"

Barling started and flushed.

"I never said—"

"*Mais, non, mais, non!* You said nothing. But it was so, was it not?"

"I fell in love with her—yes. Lytcham Roche was pleased about it. It fitted in with his ideas for her."

"And mademoiselle herself?"

"I told you—she's the devil incarnate."

"I comprehend. She has her own ideas of amusement, is it not so? But Captain Marshall, where does he come in?"

"Well, she's been seeing a lot of him. People talked. Not that I think there's anything in it. Another scalp, that's all."

Poirot nodded.

"But supposing that there had been something in it—well, then, it might explain why M. Lytcham Roche wanted to proceed cautiously."

"You do understand, don't you, that there's no earthly reason for suspecting Marshall of defalcation."

"*Oh, parfaitement, parfaitement!* It might be an affair of a forged check with someone in the household involved. This young Mr. Dalehouse, who is he?"

"A nephew."

"He will inherit, yes?"

"He's a sister's son. Of course he might take the name—there's not a Lytcham Roche left."

"I see."

"The place isn't actually entailed, though it's always gone from father to son. I've always imagined that he'd leave the place to his wife for her lifetime and then perhaps to Diana if he approved of her marriage. You see, her husband could take the name."

"I comprehend," said Poirot. "You have been most kind and helpful to me, monsieur. May I ask of you one thing further—to explain to Madame Lytcham Roche all that I have told you, and to beg of her that she accord me a minute?"

Sooner than he had thought likely, the door opened and Mrs. Lytcham Roche entered. She floated to a chair.

"Mr. Barling has explained everything to me," she said. "We mustn't have any scandal, of course. Though I do feel really it's fate, don't you? I mean with the mirror and everything."

"*Comment*—the mirror?"

"The moment I saw it—it seemed a symbol. Of Hubert! A curse, you know. I think old families have a curse very often. Hubert was always very strange. Lately he has been stranger than ever."

"You will forgive me for asking, madame, but you are not in any way short of money?"

"Money? I never think of money."

"Do you know what they say, madame? Those who never

think of money need a great deal of it."

He ventured a tiny laugh. She did not respond. Her eyes were far away.

"I thank you, madame," he said, and the interview came to an end.

Poirot rang, and Digby answered.

"I shall require you to answer a few questions," said Poirot. "I am a private detective sent for by your master before he died."

"A detective!" the butler gasped. "Why?"

"You will please answer my questions. As to the shot now—"

He listened to the butler's account.

"So there were four of you in the hall?"

"Yes, sir; Mr. Dalehouse and Miss Ashby and Mr. Keene came from the drawing-room."

"Where were the others?"

"The others, sir?"

"Yes, Mrs. Lytcham Roche, Miss Cleves and Mr. Barling."

"Mrs. Lytcham Roche and Mr. Barling came down later, sir."

"And Miss Cleves?"

"I think Miss Cleves was in the drawing-room, sir."

Poirot asked a few more questions, then dismissed the butler with the command to request Miss Cleves to come to him.

She came immediately, and he studied her attentively in view of Barling's revelations. She was certainly beautiful in her white satin frock with the rosebud on the shoulder.

He explained the circumstances which had brought him to Lytcham Close, eyeing her very closely, but she showed only what seemed to be genuine astonishment, with no signs of uneasiness. She spoke of Marshall indifferently with tepid approval. Only at mention of Barling did she approach animation.

"That man's a crook," she said sharply. "I told the Old Man so, but he wouldn't listen—went on putting money into his rotten concerns."

"Are you sorry, mademoiselle, that your—father is dead?"

She stared at him.

"Of course. I'm modern, you know, M. Poirot. I don't indulge in sob stuff. But I was fond of the Old Man. Though, of course, it's best for him."

"Best for him?"

"Yes. One of these days he would have had to be locked up. It was growing on him—this belief that the last Lytcham Roche of Lytcham Close was omnipotent."

Poirot nodded thoughtfully.

"I see, I see—yes, decided signs of mental trouble. By the way, you permit that I examine your little bag? It is charming—all these silk rosebuds. What was I saying? Oh, yes, did you hear the shot?"

"Oh, yes! But I thought it was a car or a poacher, or something."

"You were in the drawing-room?"

"No. I was out in the garden."

"I see. Thank you, mademoiselle. Next I would like to see M. Keene, is it not?"

"Geoffrey? I'll send him along."

Keene came in, alert and interested.

"Mr. Barling has been telling me of the reason for your being down here. I don't know that there's anything I can tell you, but if I can—"

Poirot interrupted him. "I only want to know one thing, Monsieur Keene. What was it that you stooped and picked up just before we got to the study door this evening?"

"I—" Keene half sprang up from his chair, then subsided again. "I don't know what you mean," he said lightly.

"Oh, I think you do, monsieur. You were behind me, I know, but a friend of mine he says I have eyes in the back of my head. You picked up something and you put it in the right-hand pocket of your dinner jacket."

There was a pause. Indecision was written plainly on Keene's handsome face. At last he made up his mind.

"Take your choice, M. Poirot," he said, and leaning forward he turned his pocket inside out. There was a cigarette holder, a handkerchief, a tiny silk rosebud, and a little gold match box.

A moment's silence and then Keene said, "As a matter of fact it was this." He picked up the match box. "I must have dropped it earlier in the evening."

"I think not," said Poirot.

"What do you mean?"

"What I say. I, monsieur, am a man of tidiness, of method, of order. A match box on the ground, I should see it and pick it up—a match box of this size, assuredly I should see it! No, monsieur, I think it was something very much smaller—such as this, perhaps."

He picked up the little silk rosebud.

"From Miss Cleves's bag, I think?"

There was a moment's pause, then Keene admitted it with a laugh.

"Yes, that's so. She—gave it to me last night."

"I see," said Poirot, and at the moment the door opened and a tall fair-haired man in a lounge suit strode into the room.

"Keene—what's all this? Lytcham Roche shot himself? Man, I can't believe it. It's incredible."

"Let me introduce you," said Keene, "to M. Hercule Poirot." The other started. "He will tell you all about it." And he left the room, banging the door.

"M. Poirot"—John Marshall was all eagerness—"I'm most awfully pleased to meet you. It is a bit of luck your being down here. Lytcham Roche never told me you were coming. I'm a most frightful admirer of yours, sir."

A disarming young man, thought Poirot—not so young,

either, for there was gray hair at the temples and lines in the forehead. It was the voice and manner that gave the impression of boyishness.

"The police—"

"They are here now, sir. I came up with them on hearing the news. They don't seem particularly surprised. Of course, he was mad as a hatter, but even then—"

"Even then you are surprised at his committing suicide?"

"Frankly, yes. I shouldn't have thought that—well, that Lytcham Roche could have imagined the world getting on without him."

"He has had money troubles of late, I understand?"

Marshall nodded.

"He speculated. Wildcat schemes of Barling's."

Poirot said quietly, "I will be very frank. Had you any reason to suppose that Mr. Lytcham Roche suspected you of tampering with your accounts?"

Marshall stared at Poirot in a kind of ludicrous bewilderment. So ludicrous was it that Poirot was forced to smile.

"I see that you are utterly taken aback, Captain Marshall."

"Yes, indeed. The idea's ridiculous."

"Ah! Another question. He did not suspect you of robbing him of his adopted daughter?"

"Oh, so you know about me and Di?" He laughed in an embarrassed fashion.

"It is so, then?"

Marshall nodded.

"But the old man didn't know anything about it. Di wouldn't have him told. I suppose she was right. He'd have gone up like a—a basketful of rockets. I should have been chucked out of a job, and that would have been that."

"And instead what was your plan?"

"Well, upon my word, sir, I hardly know. I left things to

Di. She said she'd fix it. As a matter of fact I was looking out for a job. If I could have got one I would have chucked this up."

"And mademoiselle would have married you? But M. Lytcham Roche might have stopped her allowance. Mademoiselle Diana is, I should say, fond of money."

Marshall looked rather uncomfortable.

"I'd have tried to make it up to her, sir."

Geoffrey Keene came into the room. "The police are just going and would like to see you, M. Poirot."

"*Merci.* I will come."

In the study were a stalwart inspector and the police surgeon.

"Mr. Poirot?" said the inspector. "We've heard of you, sir. I'm Inspector Reeves."

"You are most amiable," said Poirot, shaking hands. "You do not need my co-operation, no?" He gave a little laugh.

"Not this time, sir. All plain sailing."

"The case is perfectly straightforward, then?" demanded Poirot.

"Absolutely. Door and window locked, key of door in dead man's pocket. Manner very strange the past few days. No doubt about it."

"Everything quite—natural?"

The doctor grunted.

"Must have been sitting at a damned queer angle for the bullet to have hit that mirror. But suicide's a queer business."

"You found the bullet?"

"Yes, here." The doctor held it out. "Near the wall below the mirror. Pistol was Mr. Roche's own. Kept it in the drawer of the desk always. Something behind it all, I daresay, but what that is we shall never know."

Poirot nodded.

The body had been carried to a bedroom. The police

now took their leave. Poirot stood at the front door looking after them. A sound made him turn. Harry Dalehouse was close behind him.

"Have you, by any chance, a strong flashlight, my friend?" asked Poirot.

"Yes, I'll get it for you."

When he returned with it Joan Ashby was with him.

"You may accompany me if you like," said Poirot graciously.

He stepped out of the front door and turned to the right, stopping before the study window. About six feet of grass separated it from the path. Poirot bent down, playing the flashlight on the grass. He straightened himself and shook his head.

"No," he said, "not there."

Then he paused and slowly his figure stiffened. On either side of the grass was a deep flower border. Poirot's attention was focused on the right-hand border, full of Michaelmas daisies and dahlias. His torch was directed on the front of the bed. Distinct on the soft mold were footprints.

"Four of them," murmured Poirot. "Two going toward the window, two coming from it."

"A gardener," suggested Joan.

"But no, mademoiselle, but no. Employ your eyes. These shoes are small, dainty, high-heeled, the shoes of a woman. Mademoiselle Diana mentioned having been out in the garden. Do you know if she went downstairs before you did, mademoiselle?"

Joan shook her head.

"I can't remember. I was in such a hurry because the gong went, and I thought I'd heard the first one. I do seem to remember that her room door was open as I went past, but I'm not sure. Mrs. Lytcham Roche's was shut, I know."

"I see," said Poirot.

Something in his voice made Harry look up sharply, but

Poirot was merely frowning gently to himself.

In the doorway they met Diana Cleves.

"The police have gone," she said. "It's all—over."

She gave a deep sigh.

"May I request one little word with you, mademoiselle?"

She led the way into the morning room, and Poirot followed, shutting the door.

"Well?" She looked a little surprised.

"One little question, mademoiselle. Were you tonight at any time in the flower border outside the study window?"

"Yes." She nodded. "About seven o'clock and again just before dinner."

"I do not understand," he said.

"I can't see that there is anything to 'understand,' as you call it," she said coldly. "I was picking Michaelmas daisies —for the table. I always do the flowers. That was about seven o'clock."

"And afterward—later?"

"Oh, that! As a matter of fact I dropped a spot of hair oil on my dress—just on the shoulder here. It was just as I was ready to come down. I didn't want to change the dress. I remembered I'd seen a late rose in bud in the border. I ran out and picked it and pinned it in. See—" She came close to him and lifted the head of the rose. Poirot saw the minute grease spot. She remained close to him, her shoulder almost brushing his.

"And what time was this?"

"Oh, about ten minutes past eight, I suppose."

"You did not—try the window?"

"I believe I did. Yes, I thought it would be quicker to go in that way. But it was fastened."

"I see." Poirot drew a deep breath. "And the shot," he said, "where were you when you heard that? Still in the flower border?"

"Oh, no; it was two or three minutes later, just before I came in by the side door."

"Do you know what this is, mademoiselle?"

On the palm of his hand he held out the tiny silk rosebud. She examined it coolly.

"It looks like a rosebud off my little evening bag. Where did you find it?"

"It was in Mr. Keene's pocket," said Poirot dryly. "Did you give it to him, mademoiselle?"

"Did he tell you I gave it to him?"

Poirot smiled.

"When did you give it to him, mademoiselle?"

"Last night."

"Did he warn you to say that, mademoiselle?"

"What do you mean?" she asked angrily.

But Poirot did not answer. He strode out of the room and into the drawing-room. Barling, Keene, and Marshall were there. He went straight up to them.

"Messieurs," he said brusquely, "will you follow me to the study?"

He passed out into the hall and addressed Joan and Harry.

"You, too, I pray of you. And will somebody request madame to come? I thank you. Ah! And here is the excellent Digby. Digby, a little question, a very important little question. Did Miss Cleves arrange some Michaelmas daisies before dinner?"

The butler looked bewildered.

"Yes, sir, she did."

"You are sure?"

"Quite sure, sir."

"*Très bien.* Now—come, all of you."

Inside the study he faced them.

"I have asked you to come here for a reason. The case is over, the police have come and gone. They say Mr. Lytcham Roche has shot himself. All is finished." He paused. "But I, Hercule Poirot, say that it is not finished."

As startled eyes turned to him the door opened and Mrs.

Lytcham Roche floated into the room.

"I was saying, madame, that this case is not finished. It is a matter of the psychology. Mr. Lytcham Roche, he had the *manie de grandeur,* he was a king. Such a man does not kill himself. No, no, he may go mad, but he does not kill himself. Mr. Lytcham Roche did not kill himself." He paused. "He was killed."

"Killed?" Marshall gave a short laugh. "Alone in a room with the door and window locked?"

"All the same," said Poirot stubbornly, "he was killed."

"And got up and locked the door or shut the window afterward, I suppose," said Diana cuttingly.

"I will show you something," said Poirot, going to the window. He turned the handle of the French windows and then pulled gently.

"See, they are open. Now I close them, but without turning the handle. Now the window is closed but not fastened. Now!"

He gave a short jarring blow and the handle turned, shooting the bolt down into its socket.

"You see?" said Poirot softly. "It is very loose, this mechanism. It could be done from outside quite easily."

He turned, his manner grim.

"When that shot was fired at twelve minutes past eight, there were four people in the hall. Four people have an alibi. Where were the other three? You, madame? In your room. You, Monsieur Barling. Were you, too, in your room?"

"I was."

"And you, mademoiselle, were in the garden. So you have admitted."

"I don't see—" began Diana.

"Wait." He turned to Mrs. Lytcham Roche. "Tell me, madame, have you any idea of how your husband left his money?"

"Hubert read me his will. He said I ought to know. He

left me three thousand a year chargeable on the estate, and the dower house or the town house, whichever I preferred. Everything else he left to Diana, on condition that if she married her husband must take the name."

"Ah!"

"But then he made a codicil thing—a few weeks ago, that was."

"Yes, madame?"

"He still left it all to Diana, but on condition that she married Mr. Barling. If she married anyone else, it was all to go to his nephew, Harry Dalehouse."

"But the codicil was only made a few weeks ago," purred Poirot. "Mademoiselle may not have known of that." He stepped forward accusingly. "Mademoiselle Diana, you want to marry Captain Marshall, do you not? Or is it Mr. Keene?"

She walked across the room and put her arm through Marshall's sound one.

"Go on," she said.

"I will put the case against you, mademoiselle. You loved Captain Marshall. You also loved money. Your adopted father he would never have consented to your marrying Captain Marshall, but if he dies you are fairly sure that you get everything. So you go out, you step over the flower border to the window which is open, you have with you the pistol which you have taken from the writing-table drawer. You go up to your victim talking amiably. You fire. You drop the pistol by his hand, having wiped it and then pressed his fingers on it. You go out again, shaking the window till the bolt drops. You come into the house. Is that how it happened? I am asking you, mademoiselle?"

"No," Diana screamed. "No—no!"

He looked at her, then he smiled.

"No," he said, "it was not like that. It might have been so—it is plausible—it is possible—but it cannot have been like that for two reasons. The first reason is that you picked

Michaelmas daisies at seven o'clock, the second arises from something that mademoiselle here told me." He turned toward Joan, who stared at him in bewilderment. He nodded encouragement.

"But yes, mademoiselle. You told me that you hurried downstairs because you thought it was the second gong sounding, having already heard the first."

He shot a rapid glance round the room.

"You do not see what that means?" he cried. "You do not see. Look! Look!" He sprang forward to the chair where the victim had sat. "Did you notice how the body was? Not sitting square to the desk—no, sitting sideways to the desk, facing the window. Is that a natural way to commit suicide? *Jamais, jamais!* You write your apologia 'sorry' on a piece of paper—you open the drawer, you take out the pistol, you hold it to your head and you fire. That is the way of suicide. But now consider murder! The victim sits at his desk, the murderer stands beside him—talking. And talking still—fires. Where does the bullet go then?" He paused. "Straight through the head, through the door if it is open, and so—hits the gong.

"Ah! you begin to see? That was the first gong—heard only by mademoiselle, since her room is above.

"What does our murderer do next? Shuts the door, locks it, puts the key in the dead man's pocket, then turns the body sideways in the chair, presses the dead man's fingers on the pistol and then drops it by his side, cracks the mirror on the wall as a final spectacular touch—in short, 'arranges' his suicide. Then out through the window, the bolt is shaken home, the murderer steps not on the grass, where footprints must show, but on the flower bed, where they can be smoothed out behind him, leaving no trace. Then back into the house, and at twelve minutes past eight, when he is alone in the drawing-room, he fires a service revolver out of the drawing-room window and dashes out into the hall. Is that how you did it, Mr. Geoffrey Keene?"

"Well—it's obvious, isn't it? This cry for help occupies a perfectly definite place and time in space. The place is the vicinity of that cottage and the time is twenty-five minutes past seven."

"Yes, but why should I be the one to hear it? I don't believe in ghosts and all that spook stuff—spirits rapping and all the rest of it. Why should I hear the damned thing?"

"Ah! That we can't tell at present. It's a curious thing that many of the best mediums are made out of confirmed skeptics. It isn't the people who are interested in occult phenomena who get the manifestations. Some people see and hear things that other people don't—we don't know why, and nine times out of ten they don't want to see or hear them, and are convinced that they are suffering from delusions—just as you were. It's like electricity. Some substances are good conductors, and for a long time we didn't know why, and had to be content just to accept the fact. Nowadays we do know why. Some day, no doubt, we shall know why you hear this thing and I and the girl don't. Everything's governed by natural law, you know—there's no such thing really as the supernatural. Finding out the laws that govern so-called psychic phenomena is going to be a tough job—but every little helps."

"But what am I going to do?" asked Jack.

Lavington chuckled.

"Practical, I see. Well, my young friend, you are going to have a good breakfast and get off to the city without worrying your head further about things you don't understand. I, on the other hand, am going to poke about, and see what I can find out about that cottage back there. That's where the mystery centers, I dare swear."

Jack rose to his feet.

"Right, sir. I'm on, but, I say—"

"Yes?"

Jack flushed awkwardly.

"I'm sure the girl's all right," he muttered.

Lavington looked amused.

"You didn't tell me she was a pretty girl! Well, cheer up, I think the mystery started before her time."

Jack arrived home that evening in a perfect fever of curiosity. He was by now pinning his faith blindly to Lavington. The doctor had accepted the matter so naturally, had been so matter-of-fact and unperturbed by it, that Jack was impressed.

He found his new friend waiting for him in the hall when he came down for dinner, and the doctor suggested that they should dine together at the same table.

"Any news, sir?" asked Jack anxiously.

"I've collected the life history of Heather Cottage all right. It was tenanted first by an old gardener and his wife. The old man died, and the old woman went to her daughter. Then a builder got hold of it, and modernized it with great success, selling it to a city gentleman who used it for week-ends. About a year ago, he sold it to some people called Turner—Mr. and Mrs. Turner. They seem to have been rather a curious couple from all I can make out. He was an Englishman, his wife was popularly supposed to be partly Russian, and was a very handsome, exotic-looking woman. They lived very quietly, seeing no one, and hardly ever going outside the cottage garden. The local rumor goes that they were afraid of something—but I don't think we ought to rely on that.

"And then suddenly one day they departed, cleared out one morning early, and never came back. The agents here got a letter from Mr. Turner, written from London, instructing him to sell the place as quickly as possible. The furniture was sold off, and the house itself was sold to a Mr. Mauleverer. He only actually lived in it a fortnight—then he advertised it to be let furnished. The people who have it now are a consumptive French professor and his daughter. They have been there just ten days."

Jack digested this in silence.

"I don't see that that gets us any forrader," he said at last. "Do you?"

"I rather want to know more about the Turners," said Lavington quietly. "They left very early in the morning, you remember. As far as I can make out, nobody actually saw them go. Mr. Turner has been seen since—but I can't find anybody who has seen Mrs. Turner."

Jack paled.

"It can't be—you don't mean—"

"Don't excite yourself, young man. The influence of anyone at the point of death—and especially of violent death—upon their surroundings is very strong. Those surroundings might conceivably absorb that influence, transmitting it in turn to a suitably tuned receiver—in this case yourself."

"But why me?" murmured Jack rebelliously. "Why not someone who could do some good?"

"You are regarding the force as intelligent and purposeful, instead of blind and mechanical. I do not believe myself in earth-bound spirits, haunting a spot for one particular purpose. But the thing I have seen, again and again, until I can hardly believe it to be pure coincidence, is a kind of blind groping toward justice—a subterranean moving of blind forces, always working obscurely toward that end—"

He shook himself—as though casting off some obsession that preoccupied him, and turned to Jack with a ready smile.

"Let us banish the subject—for tonight at all events," he suggested.

Jack agreed readily enough, but did not find it so easy to banish the subject from his own mind.

During the week-end, he made vigorous inquiries of his own, but succeeded in eliciting little more than the doctor had done. He had definitely given up playing golf before breakfast.

The next link in the chain came from an unexpected quarter. On getting back one day, Jack was informed that a young lady was waiting to see him. To his intense surprise it proved to be the girl of the garden—the pansy girl, as he always called her in his own mind. She was very nervous and confused.

"You will forgive me, monsieur, for coming to seek you like this? But there is something I want to tell you—I—"

She looked around uncertainly.

"Come in here," said Jack promptly, leading the way into the now deserted ladies' drawing-room of the hotel, a dreary apartment, with a good deal of red plush about it. "Now, sit down, Miss—Miss—"

"Marchaud, monsieur. Felise Marchaud."

"Sit down, Mademoiselle Marchaud, and tell me all about it."

Felise sat down obediently. She was dressed in dark green today, and the beauty and charm of the proud little face was more evident than ever. Jack's heart beat faster as he sat down beside her.

"It is like this," explained Felise. "We have been here but a short time, and from the beginning we hear the house—our so sweet little house—is haunted. No servant will stay in it. That does not matter so much—me, I can do the *ménage* and cook easily enough."

Angel, thought the infatuated young man. *She's wonderful*. But he maintained an outward semblance of businesslike attention.

"This talk of ghosts, I think it is all folly—that is until four days ago. Monsieur, four nights running, I have had the same dream. A lady stands there—she is beautiful, tall, and very fair. In her hands she holds a blue china jar. She is distressed—very distressed, and continually she holds out the jar to me, as though imploring me to do something with it. But alas! She cannot speak, and I—I do not know what she asks. That was the dream for the first two nights